C IS FOR COLT

ASSASSINZ ROMANTIC THRILLERS

E.L. SNOW

ASSASINZ
ROMANTIC THRILLERS

Published by Curtain Call Press

ISBN: 978-0-9984830-7-8

Publisher's Note: This is a work of fiction. Names, characters, places, and incidents are a product of the author's imagination. Locales and public names are sometimes used for atmospheric purposes. Any resemblance to actual people, living or dead, or to businesses, companies, events, institutions, or locales is completely coincidental.

Man at Filthy New Mexico Compound Was Training Kids to Commit School Shootings, Prosecutors Say
    CBS — August 8, 2018

New Mexico Compound: Man Allegedly Trained Captive Children to Commit School Shootings
    Newsweek — August 8, 2018

Man Arrested at 'Extremist Muslim' New Mexico Compound Was Training Kids to Commit School Shootings: Documents
    Fox News — August 8, 2018

It's my lucky day.

Which it really should be, seeing as it's my twenty-third birthday.

There he is, Mr. Luscious, striding into view with an easy gait. My heart backflips. Lanky and light-haired, he isn't the best-looking guy I've run across. But, even with all the celebrities I've met, something about his ramrod spine and sense of purpose catapults him high on the list.

Mr. Luscious, indeed.

I flinch at my thoughts. I sound like a tween in the first flush of a crush when I'm anything but. I'm repeating my junior year of college for the third time. And, since I'm skipping class so I can be here, watching Mr. Luscious exit a parking garage, there's a better than good chance I'll be repeating my junior year for the fourth time when the spring semester ends soon. I don't even want to think about how my parents will freak out if that happens. They might stop talking to me.

I squint. The mid-April late-afternoon sun has cast a white haze over my windshield, which makes it hard to keep a bead on him. I follow the undulation of his movements as he walks through the wide mouth of the garage onto Sixth Street, Austin's most happening strip. The noise fills in what my eyes can't see. Although it's not even five o'clock, the bars and restaurants are overflowing with people unwinding with happy-hour drinks and half-price appetizers.

I could be one of them, but instead, I've set myself one goal for today—meet Mr. Luscious. It seems a more interesting way to spend my birthday than listening to my ancient professor drone about Valley Forge. Plus, what a fabulous present if I do, in fact, succeed.

Mr. Luscious turns a corner as I curse under my breath. I should have started following him sooner. I smile big, fluffing my hair with one hand while pushing the car door open with the other.

Time to have fun.

I run-walk as fast as I can in my shiny gold sandals with heels long and sharp like knitting needles. Then, I skid on a pebble, which causes my ankle to roll over. My body tips, but I catch my balance, barely saving myself from a nasty fall.

Pay attention, Libby, I say to myself as I roll my eyes at my footwear choice. If only I'd stuck with the comfy flip-flops I'd been wearing earlier. But I wanted to look good, and I'd been pleased with how the sandals made my legs look long and lean—something I hoped Mr. Luscious would notice too.

Now, actually in them, they just pinch my toes and throw off my balance. There's nothing sexy about that.

As I pull up to the garage's exit, a rectangle of white plastic catches my eye. It's one of those badges employees use to swipe in and out of buildings. I narrow my eyes. Light hair. A handsome nose. A steady gaze.

It's Mr. Luscious' badge. I swoop down and grab it as my pulse quickens.

I've got my in, I say to myself as I glance down to get his name.

Marvin Martins, I read and then frown.

Mr. Luscious is named . . . Marvin Martins. How dorky. I'd

assumed someone that good looking would have a more elegant name like—

Head in the clouds, I've lost sight of Mr. Luscious. I peek at the crowd on Sixth Street. The blond hair of Mr. Luscious, aka Marvin Martins, glints tantalizingly before he's absorbed into a crowd outside a dueling piano bar. I take off in his direction.

For a few minutes, I pick my way through the crowd, catching glimpses of his rangy frame. Then, a girl steps right in front of me, lifting her phone to take a picture. By the time she's done, I've lost sight of him.

I sigh. *This is dumb. I am dumb.*

I should blow off the mission, return to my apartment, and start the paper that's due tomorrow for Politics through Film, a class so easy I have no excuse not to pass it.

I don't. Instead, I redouble my efforts, elbowing my way through the throng, excusing myself with a dippy smile and an effusive *pardon me*.

Texas—the state where you can get away with anything as long as you do it politely enough.

After a few minutes, I'm ready to turn back. Mr. Luscious has disappeared, and the crowd keeps getting denser. I can't even lift my arms to the side.

"What's going on?" I ask the girl next to me.

She flips her ponytail over her shoulder. "Alexander Benoit is what's going on." She points at a rustic-looking bar with a big, beamed roof. "He's filming a scene in there for a movie about the Stephen F. Austin High School shooting. He's playing that guy, Chris Whatshisname, who the shooter made pick between his disabled brother and his girlfriend." Her voice goes breathless. "After he's done, "He is going to stay for a drink and sign autographs."

That explains the crush of people. Alexander is one of the hottest actors right now, his blue eyes lighting up a million screens every day.

I laugh to myself. I know Alexander—a perk of having a dad

like mine. I don't know him well, but I do know why he's staying to have a drink. He's asexual. He has zero romantic feelings toward anybody, man or woman. He despises being touched, and in his movies, he has a stand-in for his romantic scenes. That, though, is not a quality that makes hordes of panting women line up for movie tickets.

I want to tell the ponytailed teenybopper the truth: Alexander needs a few tabloid pictures of him living up the life of booze and babes to quell the rumors and reassert his status as a leading man, both on-screen and off.

I don't because, through the waving arms and lolling heads, Mr. Luscious is pushing his way toward the front. I redouble my efforts and launch myself until I end up beside him. We're stuck behind a wall of bodyguards, people pressing against us on the other three sides. Even with the stink of sweat and eagerness surrounding me, I'm smiling. If Mr. Luscious doesn't work out, I can catch up with Alexander. We'll have a drink, and I can find out how he's navigating the treacherous sea of celebrities where it's swim or be sunk by another, more ambitious actor.

"Mr. Martins?" I ask in my best finishing school voice.

He ignores me.

I try again.

Same result.

I tug the sleeve of his denim jacket, determined to make him notice me. "Excuse me, but I found something of yours." Then, I slide in front of him and stick out my chest as best as I can. The effort is probably wasted because of the limited space, but I'm committed to giving it my all.

Marvin Martins ignores me for the third time, which is unfortunate. Because now that I'm up close and in his personal space, I like him more than ever. He radiates this leonine energy— sure-footed and utterly confident. There's also something about the way his blond hair dips over his brow that seems familiar, like I know him even though I don't.

Nobody forgets a man like this.

I lift his work badge in front of his eyes. "Take a look at this."

He brushes it away. "Not mine."

"It most certainly is yours." I push it in front of him. "See."

He tries to step away from me, but the crowd pushes him back in front of me. I use the opportunity to press the badge against his face, covering his eyes. "You're Marvin Martins, and I found your identification in the parking—"

POP.

I recognize the sound, just like everyone else in America, but I've never heard it in real life. Instead of ducking for cover or running for my life like everyone else is doing, I freeze. The work badge slips from my fingers as my terrified eyes meet Marvin Martins' angry ones.

POP. POP. POP.

The gunshots are coming faster from the bar to us—the sitting ducks that are the crowd.

I waver back and forth on my ridiculously high heels.

I'm going to die.

I brace myself, anticipating the smack of a bullet against my skin, my shocked gasp, the icy and then the fiery path it will rip through my body. As I crumple to the ground, my heart will beat for the last time.

Better me than most of these people. I admit the truth one confronts at the end of a not particularly useful or generous life.

2

I'm still standing when a bullet whizzes by my ear. Although it doesn't hit me, my body folds like an accordion from the shock. Marvin Martins grabs me, and in something akin to a dance move, he places his hands under my armpits and rotates me a quarter turn until he's dipping me.

Gently, he lowers me to the pavement and positions himself on top of me.

"Don't move," he says.

I open my mouth to respond, but nothing comes out. I try again and manage a squeak that sounds like yes. For seconds that feel like hours, I lie under Marvin Martins' body, too scared to move, to breathe.

Around me, the world is in chaos. Although I can't see, I can hear, and the sounds are horrifying, especially the ones I've never heard before but can identify.

Thud, thud, thud: those are the feet, sprinting away.

"*Oh, God, no*": those are the screams of horror.

Thump, thump, thump: those are the bodies falling.

For what feels like hours, nothing changes, just more thuds, screams, and thumps. Slowly, then quickly, the atmosphere changes. The footsteps slow, the screams soften, and the thumps mercifully stop.

I twitch under Marvin Martins. I should get up. There will be cops who need statements and newscasters who want interviews. I can do both, fulfill my duty to the public to inform them about the horror of being present at a mass shooting. Then, I'll go to the airport and take the first flight home.

After hearing about this, Mommy and Daddy should be happy to see me. We'll finally mend the rift that has grown canyon-sized over the last few years.

Next to me, a woman is sobbing her wails almost animalistic in their grief.

"Greg," she cries. "Get up. We're supposed to have dinner at that swanky sushi place. You know how snippy the hostess gets if you're even a minute late, and it's already five past our reservation. So, Greg, you have to get up."

Although Marvin Martins is still lying on top of me, limiting my range of mobility, I turn my head toward the voice.

I gasp as my eyes meet the gray-eyed, unseeing gaze of a man who is clearly dead. My eyes lower to avoid the way his face is frozen into a fright mask.

I recoil. Blood pools between us, pumping from the wound in his chest where a bullet struck him.

A couple of inches more to the left, and I would have taken that bullet.

The woman who loves Greg has realized he will not be joining her at the swanky sushi restaurant. Ever again. Sobbing, she pulls his blood-splattered body to hers and cradles his head in her lap.

If that had been me, considering how furious my parents have been with me recently, my mother would have squeezed out a few tears before going shopping for a fancy wardrobe in black. Daddy might have had his calls held for a day or so, but business wouldn't wait for more than that. As for my friends in name only, they might care enough to post a banal one-liner to a social media account, but I'd be forgotten soon after.

No one would care.

Not that I've given anyone much reason to care, and I only have myself to blame for that.

I'm surprised from my depressing but true thoughts when Marvin Martins rolls off me and extends a hand. The gentlemanly gesture is at odds with his expression, which is livid, like he blames me.

What did I do? I think, confused. *No one knew there was going to be a mass shooting.*

"Come with me," he says.

Too shocked to do anything except follow, I place my hand in his as he hoists me to my feet. At a whip-fast speed, he leads me through the fray. I'm too stunned to respond rationally, but I know one thing—the blood-splattered images will wake me up for years to come.

I try to keep up with Marvin Martins, but my stupid heels slow me down. Plus, my legs won't stop wobbling. They refuse to support my weight, and before I know it, I've tripped over a gaggle of girls who are sitting stricken in a clump.

"We should get a picture," one says. "So we won't forget."

So you won't forget?

You think you'll be lucky enough to forget?

With somber faces, they crowd together as a girl snaps a picture with her phone.

"Posting," the picture-taker says.

I'm so dumbfounded that I can't catch myself, and I fall into them. Marvin Martins yanks me up. He steadies me and then looks at my feet. With an annoyed sigh, he reaches down, picks up my legs, and swings me into his arms like I'm a baby.

"It's easier this way," he says.

It must because I'm in a daze, but I don't challenge his actions. Instead, I go limp. I am only grateful he's taking me away from this horror. I lean my head against his chest that's rippled with muscles. His heart beats against my cheek. Its regular rhythm and the warmth of his body comfort me.

He hopscotches through the mess until we're a long way away

from the shooting, the only people around us a few innocent souls who don't know what's happened and still anticipate a night of fun.

Now that we're in a safe area—not that I'll ever feel safe again—I drop my weight in anticipation of him letting me go.

My lips begin to form the words *thank you*, but the phrase never leaves my mouth because Marvin Martins has quickened his pace into a sprint.

"I'm okay," I say as he flies through the night, taking the back streets. "I can walk."

"Not necessary." He turns the corner, the parking garage ahead.

How did he know that I drove here, that my car is in this parking garage? I ask myself.

Too overwrought to think through it all, I shelve that thought and focus on the more important one—getting myself home.

"My car is right there. You can let me down." My tone has a pleading edge. I want to get out of here, not make polite conversation.

"I wouldn't feel right about that," he says. "Let me see you home."

3

I let Marvin Martins see me home. Which is to say I unlock the car with my right index finger while ignoring his raised eyebrows as he takes in my hot-pink convertible that I call the Barbie-mobile. In a colorless voice, I point out the keyless ignition and then issue directions.

It's crazy letting him drive me home, but my sensibilities are dulled, almost nonexistent. I can't think logically.

All I can do is feel. The emotions, though, careening through me are different from my typical ones, which are a pastel wash, ranging from minor frustration to mild satisfaction. Now, my feelings have points, edges, colors that are smeared with blood and ash. They sound like screams and sirens. They hurt like nothing before.

As we drive through the familiar streets, I can't stop remembering Greg's lifeless eyes, his bawling wife, the bullet that whizzed past me, a little too left to take me down.

Marvin Martins slows as he approaches my apartment complex. It's one of those new-construction buildings that has every amenity under the sun, including an Olympic pool, a state-of-the-art gym, and a concierge service. In the parking garage, the evening guard is on duty, but he barely looks up as we pull up.

I peek around, so he can see my face and press the button to let the gate up.

The gate is a joke, nothing more than a bar that raises and lowers. The guard, a nice-enough grandpa type, is even more so. If there were a mass shooting here, he would get the first bullet but not the last.

The guard waves us through, his attention on the black-and-white television in his booth. Bile spurts up my throat. The station is tuned to the aftermath of the shooting. I look away to avoid traumatizing myself more.

Marvin Martins parks, jumps out, jogs to my side, and opens the door. I should be charmed by his gentlemanly gesture, but instead, I collapse into the seat. I'm too exhausted to move. All I want is to fall into a sleep so deep that, maybe, when I wake up, the shooting will have faded in its horror and intensity.

"Leave me here," I say. "I'll be fine." I gesture to the guard whose bald head is glowing under the fluorescent lights like a freshly shined shoe. "There's security."

Marvin Martins pulls back and gazes at me, his blond hair flopping in his eyes. Once again, I can't ignore the feeling that I know him from somewhere.

But I don't. I may not be any great shakes at school, but I do have a good memory for who've I met and where I've met them. When I was still in my parents' good graces, my dad would take me to parties so that I could remind him of the people he'd met before.

"That's not a good idea," he says. "No offense to your security."

"You did your Boy Scout act," I say tiredly. "Now go. Please."

"I don't get my badge until I make sure you're safe and sound in your apartment." His face is set; his eyes are determined.

I shrug and throw my hand in his. It's only a few more steps until I'm home. In silence, we ride the elevator to the penthouse. The doors slide open to my apartment that's decorated in a style I've dubbed chick shtick.

Before I moved to Austin, I daydreamed about the college

12

experience that had been portrayed in a thousand or more movies: a gaggle of girlfriends, flirtations with frat boys, all-nighters, tequila shots.

So I outfitted my penthouse like these dreams had already come true with leopard-print loveseats, squashy pillows, and a throw rug in fuchsia. My cabinets groaned with martini glasses and white-wine goblets. Yet it only took a couple of weeks of classes before it became clear that the gulf between the Texas belles and me was too vast to cross. I was never joining a sorority, much less having girls over for cold drinks and hot gossip.

So that's how I ended up with a chair in the shape of a high heel. Because I'm that ridiculous. I always assume that, just because I believe it, then I will achieve it even though nothing in my life supports it.

Normally, I would cringe at having a hot guy like Marvin Martins see my cheesy home decor, but I don't care right now. I kick off my high heels and turn to face him. He's staring at an end table clustered with photos of my family. Most of them are a few years old since I haven't seen my parents in almost two years, right after I failed my junior year for the first time.

I sigh.

Marvin Martins' eyes are fixed on a picture from my sixteenth birthday where my dad, white-haired and regal-looking, is handing me the keys to my first car.

He picks up the photo and narrows his eyes at it. "Is that your father?"

I nod.

"He looks familiar."

"That's because you've seen him everywhere: television, newspapers, awards shows, gossip columns." I say it nonchalantly although, internally, I'm grousing. I just want to be alone, not get waylaid by some starstruck dude.

"What's his name?" Marvin Martins' tone is casual, but his eyes are boring into mine.

"Whip Wainwright. He's the owner of Whip Media," I say. "I'm Libby Wainwright."

He nods slightly, as if I've verified what he already knew although why would he know that? He puts the photo back and grabs the card next to it—a birthday greeting from my parents, which they signed with no personal wishes. That had stung.

It had been a first. Usually, both of them included long paragraphs about health and happiness. I swipe at my eyes before pulling the card from Marvin Martins' hands.

"Just a birthday card," I say, squinting at it. My dad's signature looks different from what I remember. I wonder if—

"May I have a glass of water?" Marvin Martins asks, breaking off my thoughts.

"Sure." My tone is on the wrong side of polite.

In the kitchen, I grab a gigantic martini glass and empty a bottle of sparkling water into it. I toss in a couple of ice cubes since I've been too lazy to put the water bottles in the fridge, and my housekeepers don't come until the weekend. As I walk back into the living room, I cross my fingers on the stem that he'll drink and leave.

"Here you go." I thrust the glass toward him before my jaw drops, and my legs freeze mid-stride.

Marvin Martins is pointing a gun at me. The glass slips from my hand and crashes to the floor, creating a moat of water and shards around my feet.

"Did your father put you up to it?" he asks.

4

The surroundings of my apartment have gone blurry. The only thing that registers with precision is the gun. It's an antique one, like something a pioneer would carry. In between the long, silver barrel and a dark-wood grip lays a cylinder.

A revolver, I think, locating some piece of knowledge I didn't know I had. Six bullets although one is all it takes to ram a hole through someone's heart.

I stare at the gun, waiting for Marvin Martins' finger to tighten around the trigger.

"I don't want to hurt you," he says.

I lift my arms in surrender. "Take whatever you want." A tear winds down my cheek. "But, please, don't kill me."

He clears his throat.

He's uncomfortable, I think. *But why? He's the one with a gun.*

"I'm going to ask a few questions. If you tell the truth, then nothing bad will happen."

Nothing bad will happen? Plenty of bad things have already happened. Marvin Martins shooting me will just be the final rosette on a birthday cake of bad. But still, I'd like the chance to stick around for a few more birthdays to at least try to do something with my life other than chase guys when I should be in class.

I haven't had a chance to absorb that I survived a mass shooting, which might mean something in the future, but I have taken the point that if I'd been doing what I was supposed to be doing, then I wouldn't have been there.

"What was the question again?" I ask.

Slowly, enunciating every word, he says, "Did your father put you up to it?"

"My father? Up to what?"

"Stopping me."

"Stopping you from what?"

His nostrils flare. "I can't tell if you're lying or playing dumb."

"I don't know anything." The blood is leaving my hands, which are still in the air. I lower them to my side—bit by tiny bit. "For real."

"Then explain to me how Whip Wainwright's daughter just happened to follow me into a mass shooting."

"I don't know what you're talking about because I don't know who you are." My eyes widen as I understand at least one part of it. "You're not Marvin Martins, are you?"

"Never met the man."

I bite my lip. "Who are you then? And why were you pretending to be Marvin Martins?"

He laughs without humor. "Do you think I'm going to answer your questions?" He tightens his grip on the gun. "When you haven't answered mine."

I fling my arms back in the air as my heart slams against my chest. "I can't answer your questions because I don't know what you're asking. Yes, my father is Whip Wainwright, but he didn't put me up to anything beyond moving me to this cowpoke town."

"What are you doing in this cowpoke town?"

"Going to college." I hesitate and then decide I have nothing to lose and maybe something to gain by telling him the truth. "I'm trying to finish my junior year for the third time. My dad donated money to the University of Texas, so they'd take me. All they want is for me to finish college." A tear and then another drip down my cheeks. "Not that it matters. I'm failing again."

His fingers ease just a little on the trigger. "Why are you failing?"

"Because in two years, I can access my trust fund and do anything I want."

A solitary eyebrow shoots up. "A trust fund?"

"It's, uh, not small as far as I know." I stare at my feet. A huge chunk of broken glass rests next to my left foot. I rotate my foot away from the glass—slowly, gradually. I don't want to give not-Marvin Martins a reason to think I'm making a run for it.

"What's the problem, then? Can't you find a tutor to get you through the next two years?"

"I'm not dumb. College is dumb." I stop to correct myself. "College is dumb *for me*. I don't need to know anything beyond how to hire a good accountant, and I don't need college for that. Plus," I sob, the events of the last couple of years, capped off by tonight, are hitting me like an emotional bullet. "I have nothing in common with anyone here. It's lonely and boring, and all I want to do is leave."

Not Marvin Martins eyeballs me for a long time until he finally says, "So you're a rich girl who's killing time until she can be an even richer girl."

"Nailed it," I mutter as my chest tightens in contempt for myself. The truth hurts. It hurts even more when you know it's true.

"Why not forget college and take off for the south of France or backpack through Thailand?"

"I have to stay in college or be graduated if I want my dad to pay the bills until I'm twenty-five."

"Tough life." His tone is flippant, but he tilts his body toward me as if he's curious.

I flinch. His gun is that much closer to me now. I swallow and try to normalize my breathing.

"It's a waste of a life." I exhale, blinking back tears. That's the most honest thing I've ever said. When someone aims a gun at you, there's no purpose in pretending that anything other than the truth matters.

His eyes—a brown that seeps into gold near the pupil—scan me, but he stops at my neck. It's stupid, considering he can make me do anything he wants, but I appreciate that he's a gentleman.

Not-Marvin Martins lowers the gun until it points at the puddle of shattered glass and water I'm standing in. "Don't move." He shoves his gun in his waistband and then reaches over and lifts me out of the mess of broken glass. As if I'm no lighter than a handful of silk, he carries me a half dozen feet until my feet are on safe ground.

And that's how I know that, for at least this moment, I will be alive.

After that, who knows . . .

5

I'm perched on the high heel shoe chair, a bottle of sparkling water in my hand that not-Marvin Martins tossed to me a minute earlier. He has situated himself across from me, his body dwarfing the leopard-print loveseat.

I would laugh at a gunslinger sitting on such a girly sofa, but I'm way too edgy for humor. Although I haven't forgotten, will never forget the shooting, I'm more concerned right now with surviving my encounter with not-Marvin Martins.

I lift my eyes to him. He's tucked his gun into the waistband of his jeans, his fingers stroking the handle. He's not pointing it at me, but still, I shiver. The message is clear. In a second, maybe less, he could blow a hole through my heart.

And, because I can't help myself, I let my eyes drift over him. He's tall and slim but with well-carved muscles. He also seems utterly at ease with himself, his backbone straight, his gaze focused. He's the type of guy who doesn't need to compensate with money or fast cars because he knows that he himself is enough.

I shiver again, but it's not because of the gun. It's because of him, and how he, just sitting here, has made my insides skitter and pop. That's a bad combination—a very bad combination since he has all the power here.

I gulp water to buy myself time as I make a decision. I need to get him on my side, promise him whatever it is he wants. Then, at some point, he'll leave, and I'll hightail it out of Texas to the fortress in Connecticut that's my family's home and beg for entry.

But I need to get to that point, so I tip my head toward his gun.

"Is your gun an antique?"

He nods.

"Family heirloom?"

He nods again.

"What kind of gun is it?"

"A Colt."

"Is that a good gun?"

"It won the West."

I search for something else to ask, but I've got nothing. Because he gave me nothing. Well, not quite nothing. I got two nods and six words, which might as well be nothing. I think for a moment before I have a burst of inspiration.

"May I call you Colt?" I try to smile, but my lips twist into a half-grin/half-grimace. I'm not sure if this will push him the wrong way. "Seeing as your name isn't Marvin Martins."

He doesn't say anything for a minute, but then his lips tweak. It's not a full smile, but enough light shines in his eyes that I blink, overwhelmed. Something interesting is stewing beneath his good looks, something I want to know more about it.

I ditch that thought. I need to get him out of here, not think of reasons why I'd like him to stay.

"Colt," he says, drawing the word out like it's a strand of caramel.

I meet his gaze squarely. "Colt. After your gun."

"It's as good of a name as any."

I smile, feeling like I've won a tiny battle.

I push myself up from the sole of the high heel chair. "My dad didn't send me, Colt. Nobody sent me. I was there because . . ." My cheeks flush because what I'm about to say is beyond embarrassing. "I thought you were cute."

He smirks a little. "You thought I was cute?"

I fiddle with my earring, not meeting his eyes. "Yes."

"Was that the first time you followed me?"

I nod. "But not the first time I'd seen you."

"It wasn't?"

"Not by a long shot."

Colt sits and stares, waiting for me to say more.

This is mortifying. My whole body feels red and itchy, like one enormous bug bite.

"Do you remember how I said college is dumb for me?"

"I do."

"I've been blowing off classes for a while."

"To do what?" he asks.

"I hang out on Sixth Street. I drink coffee until I can start drinking wine."

"What does this have to do with me?"

"You walk by the restaurant. Every day, at the same time, in the same outfit." I tip my head toward Colt's button-down shirt, denim jacket, and jeans that hug his thighs. Through the material, his quadriceps bulge, which makes my pulse quicken.

His boots—made of a buttery leather the color of cognac—are sharp. He's absorbed the rules of good dressing. Always spend your money on shoes.

"But I went somewhere different today," he says. "How did you know where I was?"

I try to sink into the cushion of the high heel chair, but it refuses to let me hide. Instead, I stay perched against its straight back, forced to own my ridiculousness.

"I know your schedule," I say. "A few minutes before nine, you visit the coffee shop for an espresso and a prune Danish. At one, you go for a walk and, on the way back, stop at a food cart." I meet his eyes guiltily. "You really like short-rib tacos although sometimes you have a chicken burrito. You leave right at five to have a beer. I . . . well, today I went home to change, and then I planned to bump into you on your way for that beer."

"How come I've never noticed you? I have an eye for pretty girls."

I swallow. I like it way more than I should that he called me pretty. "I hide behind my laptop."

"Where do I go after my beer?"

I tug on the hem of my sundress. "That's what I was going to find out today."

"You don't know? Because you sure seem to know a lot about me."

"I know what you eat." I hesitate. "And when you like to eat it."

"Why don't you know where I go after?"

I press my lips together, trying to think of how to describe the thin line I'd drawn between people watching and people stalking.

"I know these things about you, but I didn't actively follow you to learn them."

"An explanation would be helpful."

"I would . . ." I stop to think of the right word. "Position myself in places where I could watch you without getting up to actively follow you."

My cheeks are so hot I can't believe they haven't ignited yet. I would give anything to disappear into the high heel shoe, not to emerge again until Colt leaves.

My "people watching" is about more than people watching. It relieves the unrelenting loneliness I've felt since I've moved to Texas. I chat with baristas and bartenders, and I watch a random, good-looking guy. It's not a life, but at least I don't feel like the silence is going to suffocate me.

"Why did you follow me today? Why not the day before or the day after?"

I gulp at my lameness. "It's my birthday, and I wanted to do something fun."

"That was your idea of fun?"

I bristle. "I don't have any friends here, and I'm bored of going shopping and sipping coffee. I also have a paper due tomorrow, so

I didn't want to do anything too crazy on the off chance I might write that paper."

He laughs wryly. "Anything too crazy."

"Believe me. I regret it. I wish I'd gone to class and then straight here to write my paper."

I meet his eyes squarely. "I don't know why you seem to think my dad put me up to stopping you. Stopping you do what, I'm not sure. But I'm telling you the truth. I'm a bored rich girl who chases guys because it's the best way I know to pass the time."

He holds my gaze for what feels like an eternity and a day. I'm the one to look away, too hot and humiliated to continue staring at him. If only he would leave, so I can escape his steady eyes and pointed questions.

You don't want him to leave, a little voice from my gut says. *You like him, this guy who uses only a few words to say a lot.*

Finally, right when the silence between us feels like it will go on forever, Colt speaks. "I believe you."

I exhale and fall back against the high heel, which I immediately regret because I hit with force, sliding down its slippery fabric until I'm in a pile on the floor, my arms and legs sticking out every which way.

The strain of the last few hours catches up with me, and I laugh. Not a joyful *he-he*, but a rolling thunder of *ha-has* that sounds like sobbing. Colt joins in, and together, we laugh for the longest time.

And for the first time since I've been in Texas, I feel like I've connected with someone.

Someone who pointed a gun at me just a few minutes earlier.

I let my laughter die out, remembering I have a goal now—get to parents' house, so I can start living a life that is less empty than the one I'm currently living. To that end, I throw back my shoulders as I stand and face him. "Do you have any more questions, or can we call it a—"

A shrill noise interrupts me. It's my phone, ringing insistently. Colt glances at it, then at me, his expression unreadable.

I freeze, unsure what I should do.

Reaching for it could result in the gun being pointed in my face again.

6

"Who's calling?" Colt asks.

I extend my neck until I can see the number. It's my mom, the last person in the world I want to talk to right now.

"My mother," I mutter.

Something like excitement flickers in his eyes. I shake that observation away. Why would he be excited about my mom calling? I'm clearly imagining things, a product of the drama I've experienced.

"Answer it," he says. "She's probably worried. The shooting has been all over the news."

I reach for my cell phone reluctantly as I try to remember the last time I spoke to one of my parents. Internally, I groan when I land on the memory. It was almost a year ago when my mom called to yell at me about failing my junior year for the second time.

I flush. In retrospect, I'd deserved it. My dad underwrote a new auditorium to get me into a liberal arts college in Vermont where I spent most of my time flirting with the TA for my Victorian Literature class. Instead of sitting for final exams, I'd flown to Ibiza to go clubbing.

At that point, I was going out of my mind in Vermont. It had snowed all winter, and everyone wore flannel all the time, and the towering pines trees made me feel claustrophobic. Although the calendar said it was May, the weather—a cold, slate-gray rain that fell for days on end—indicated otherwise. When my flirtation with the TA went nowhere, I made a snap decision to get out. The irony set in when I was having an even worse time in Ibiza. Although the sun was shining, the loud music in the clubs made my head pound, and the guys I met were gold-digging Eurotrash types.

By the time my mom had gotten me on the phone, weeks after I'd flunked out and maxed out my in-case-of-emergency credit card, she'd had enough. She told me not to come home or call until I had a college degree in hand.

And now I have to talk to her knowing that I'm failing again. Sour bile pours into my stomach as I anticipate how this conversation will go.

As I close my hands around the phone, it stops ringing. Exhaling, I release my grip.

"Too late," I say with a bright smile, relieved. I am not up to talking to my mom. I have literally nothing positive to tell her.

"Call her back."

"No. I'll have to tell her that I'm failing again, and I can't do that."

He arches an eyebrow. "Why not?"

The unspoken answer hangs in the air. *Libby fails out of everything. Why would she expect anything different?*

"I . . ." My voice fades because I haven't quite explained to myself how I'm going to change. For all my expensive education, I have no marketable skills beyond . . .

Beyond nothing.

I swallow and meet Colt's curious eyes.

"Something shifted in me tonight, something that made me decide to start living my life differently." I twist one of my diamond studs in my ear. "I just don't know how to do that yet."

"Your folks are worried." A muscle shifts in his jaw. "Call your mom back."

I pretend to be absorbed in drinking my water. After I finish the bottle, Colt passes me my phone. "Call her."

I stab at my phone, furiously hoping that maybe they're at a gala or dinner for a charity, and my mom will have had to return to whatever boring speech is going on.

My mom answers on the first ring. "Chab—"

I cough loudly, so Colt won't hear my mother say my real name, which is embarrassing.

"Yes, it's Libby." I wince at how thin and artificial my voice sounds.

"Are you okay, dumplin'? The news is filled with stories about the shooting in Austin. Imagine my shock when, in the corner of the screen, I see my daughter being carried by a man through the crowd. I thought you were . . ." She starts to cry.

I cut her off. "I'm fine."

"That is a relief and a mercy."

"It is, but I'm alive because a man saved me. He covered my body with his until the shooting was over." I try to keep talking over the knob in my throat as, in my head, I hear the bullet that whistled by me. "He even saw me home."

"What man is this? I am certainly indebted to him."

I sneak a peek at Colt. I can't exactly tell my mom that he's pointed a gun at me and goes by a fake name.

"His name is Marvin Martins, and I, uh, just happened to be near him when the shooting started."

I am *not* telling my mom that I chased him.

"Well, I'm grateful for his presence of mind. But why were you even there? You had class tonight." Over the course of those words, my mom's voice switches from high and worried to low and accusatory. The twang, a leftover from her childhood in coal country, stays the same throughout.

I sigh. We're going to have exactly the conversation I thought we were going to have.

"I . . . well, you know it's my birthday?"

"You know that I know that."

"Of course," I mutter.

"Now tell me why you weren't in class." My mom sighs. "Hold on. I got John on the other line."

Colt tips his head, his unanswered question hanging in the air.

"John Spencer IV is second in command at Whip Media. He comes from old money in Virginia. He'd buy out my dad if my dad would let him."

Those facts are probably the ones Colt cares about rather than my opinion, which is that I despise John Spencer IV. Although he's always been polite, his sharp white teeth and glittering eyes put me in mind of a wolf. He always acts in a passive-aggressive manner to my mom, asking her if she'd seen this opera or read this obscure literary novel when my mom watches rom-com movies and flips through movie magazines.

My mom returns to the line. "So why you weren't in class?"

"Because it was my birthday?"

"Are you tellin' me that the professor canceled class so that you could celebrate your birthday?"

"Not quite."

"Chab—"

I pretend to cough again as Colt frowns. He strides to the kitchen, and I forget pretty much everything except the way his butt fills out his jeans.

"Sure you're okay there?" my mom asks.

"Uh-huh," I mutter, still entranced by Colt as he turns the corner. He returns a few minutes later with another bottle of water, which I gulp, grateful that it distracts me from the lecture my mom has launched into.

". . . twenty-three, and you still can't delay your fun for a few hours. Nothin'—and I mean nothin'—is more important than school. Life might smack you in the face with something you don't expect, and a college degree is one way to survive the worst." She laughs sarcastically. "I've been dirt poor before, and it isn't much fun."

I tune her out as she says everything I expect. Then, I start to lie, just to get her off my case. "I've actually been going to class and doing my assignments. This was the first class I've skipped, I swear. Just you wait and see. I'm going to pass this time and with all A's to boot."

Silence stretches out between us. Finally, she sighs. "All right. I'll wait and see."

I widen my eyes at Colt to let him know that I'm going to hang up soon. He's listening intently, like he would take notes if he could.

"Your dad," he says in a low voice. "Ask to talk to him."

I do it without thinking about why he cares. "Can I talk to Daddy?"

There's no response, so I try again.

"Is Daddy around?"

My mom clears her throat. "He went to bed hours ago."

He went to bed hours ago, I repeat incredulously in my head. My dad regularly puts in eighteen-hour days. It wasn't uncommon for him to be up until early morning.

"Is he sick?" I ask. "Because I want to talk to him."

And that's the truth. I would love to hear his baritone voice and his booming laugh. In my head, he's still the strong, imposing man with a mane of white hair from my girlhood, but when I calculate his age, I blink in surprise. He's eighty.

How many years does he have left?

Probably not too many since he's existed on a steady diet of whiskey and steak since his twenties.

"Daddy's fine. Just tired." My mom's tone is hard and final.

"My dad is asleep," I say to Colt. I mess up, though, and say it too loud.

"Is someone there?" my mom asks.

I curse to myself. There's no way to extricate myself from this quagmire.

"The guy who saved my life. He was hanging out for a while to make sure I'm okay."

"That was awfully gentlemanly of him." Through the phone, I can hear the tap, tap, tap of her fingers on a keyboard.

"That's how they make them here." I wince at how corny that sounds as, beside me, Colt laughs softly.

My mom keeps me on the phone to lecture me about how important college is for my future. About halfway through, she loses the thread and begins to ramble about my childhood and all the times we were a happy family. The longer she goes, the more she veers off track and I'm not even sure if she's talking to me anymore although there's no one else for her to talk to.

"I still got that old baby doll, and I take real good care of her. You'd be—"

Finally, I've had enough, and I cut her off. "It was good talking to you, Mommy, but I'm tired. It hasn't been the best day. So good night," I whisper.

"Happy Birthday, dumplin'." She hangs up the phone.

I toss my phone on the table. "Satisfi—"

I can't get the word out because someone is pounding on the door.

7

I freeze, my nerves vibrating.

Colt keeps his gaze on me. "Who's knocking?" His tone is casual, but he places a hand over his gun.

"No clue. It's not like I have any friends who would come to check on me." I mean for it to be a joke, but it comes out all wrong, just sad and desperate.

He nods, his eyebrows pulled together as the thudding at the door continues. For a long moment, neither of us say anything.

"I want you to open the door and then say out loud who it is," Colt says.

I frown. I'm about to ask, *what if I don't know who it is*, when he anticipates my question.

"If you don't know, then say what you see." He pauses. "There's a tall man with brown hair in a black suit at the door," he chimes in a good imitation of a girl's voice.

Colt stares at me hard. "After that, scram. I'll take it from there. Do you understand?" He taps the top of his gun.

I nod as my mind races ahead to Colt blowing a hole through whoever is unlucky enough to be on the other side of my front door.

He tips his head toward the door, which is practically vibrating from being knocked so strongly. "Go."

I walk to the door, barely breathing, my heart thumping. Who is behind the door? What if it's a police officer? If it is, should I follow Colt's instructions? Or should I beg for the officer's help? Maybe I should do what Colt said regardless of who it is. After all, he has a gun. That's the one fact I know for sure.

The hammering has intensified to the point where I can't even hear my thoughts anymore. I inhale and then throw open the door.

There's no time to announce who it is because two women rush past me.

"Miss Libby, we were so worried—," says one as the other starts talking over her. "—knew you wouldn't go to class on your—"

And they're off, both talking so fast I can barely follow their thread.

"—so worried, I was praying—"

"—your father would never forgive—"

"—could have been killed—"

"—on your birthday, no less—"

I giggle as the two women burst into the room. Colt's eyebrows shoot up at the sight of the duo, who, to put it politely, are an odd couple.

"Orpita," I say to a short, plump Indian woman whose gold bangles are clanging against each other as she gestures wildly. "Xaviera," I say to the other woman, a gangly Latina who is fingering a cross around her neck. "Why are you here?"

"Because Miss Libby—" Orpita says breathlessly.

"The shooting—" Xaviera adds.

"We heard on the news—"

"On your birthday, you would—"

"Skip class, as you—"

"You always go to that restaurant on—"

"In the wrong place—"

"At the wrong time." Xaviera shoots Orpita a triumphant look because she won that round of verbal tic-tac-toe.

My eyes get wet. Someone was worried about me. Not someone, two people. Xaviera and Orpita, who I've secretly dubbed X and O, came to check on me.

X and O are my . . . I'm not sure what I should call them. Technically, X is my housecleaner, and O is my chef, both hired by my mother to look after my place and, more specifically, me.

In the beginning, I would step out when they came over on Saturdays, promptly at ten in the morning, but I started sticking around, mainly because they're better than a comedy show. For the few hours they're here, they make me feel like I have friends, even if they're the ones I have to pay.

Thinking that makes me cringe. I'm turning into my mom, who has no friends either and, thus, makes conversation with the help as her social outlet. The help indulges her, asking her questions and laughing at her jokes. But from the outside looking in, it's easy to see that they wish my mom would leave them alone to do their jobs.

Colt clears his throat, which reminds me I haven't followed a single one of his instructions.

"May I introduce you to the dynamic duo of Orpita and Xaviera," I say as if I'm announcing visiting royalty. "They help me around here with cleaning, cooking, and . . . other stuff." I'm not sure how to explain that they provide some—make that most—of my social stimulation.

"Ladies," Colt says as his eyes crinkle in suspicion.

X gasps as O widens her eyes.

"A man in the—" X fondles her cross.

"Miss Libby has a—" O shakes her bangles in the air.

"Boyfriend." X's grin might split her face in half, that's how happy she is at winning two games of verbal tic-tac-toe.

I hold up a hand before they say anything that could make me any more embarrassed.

"I was at the shooting on Sixth Street."

"We—" Orpita starts to say, but I barge in before they start talking over each other again.

33

"I'm fine, obviously. But I'm fine because this gentleman covered me with his body and then saw me home. He was just leaving, actually."

X and O exchange pointed glances as I sigh, understanding their look. They're going to meddle and probably issue a full report to my mom.

O pumps Colt's hand as X issues profuse thanks interspersed with even more profuse thanks to 'Dios mío.'"

"It was nothing," he says.

"Your name, sir. So we can thank you properly."

A pause. "Marvin Martins, but you can call me Colt," he says with a half-smile, like he's trying it on and liking the way it fits. "That's what I go by these days."

"Well, Mr. Colt, allow us to thank you. Miss Libby is the only daughter of Whip Wainwright, and he would be upset if anything happened to her," O says. "As—"

"We would be upset too," X follows up. "Mrs. Wainwright hired us to look after Libby, and he would want—"

"To make sure she can tell you thanks from him," O finishes, grinning that she beat X to the ending.

Before I can figure out what's happening, they've maneuvered Colt and me side-by-side on the leopard print loveseat. Even Colt seems overwhelmed by their flittering energy, and he accepts a glass of white wine they've uncorked, poured, and presented in record time.

Once we're settled in with wine and a dish of homemade nachos in front of us, X and O exchange satisfied grins before breaking into giggles. I close my eyes, trying and failing to pretend that my housekeepers haven't just tried to give me a birthday to remember in the most obvious fashion possible.

They've spent enough time in my home to know that I have never once entertained anyone, much less a handsome man who saved my life and then threatened it later.

Speaking of that handsome man, I stiffen at being so close to him. I feel like I'm sitting next to a lion, something fierce and proud and beautiful.

"Music," X says as O rattles her bangles. "Lights," she says.

Lights are dimmed, and a romantic song in Spanish wafts through the room. Although the only words I know in Spanish are the ones for alcohol, the singer's voice throbs with lovelorn intensity.

What sounds like the faint snap of a camera startles me, but when I look up, X and O are leaving, still talking over each other, as I look for something light to say to Colt. I need the words that will yank me from my increasing yearning for the man next to me and into an easy camaraderie with that man, so I can get rid of him and go home to parents.

Because I've decided I have a future. Barely missing a bullet does that to you.

I can't think of anything to say that isn't dumb, so I break the silence by reaching for a nacho. But, Dios mío, I'd momentarily forgotten that X and O believe in one flavor note, and it's spicy, as in clean-you-from-the-inside-out spicy. The first couple of chews aren't too bad, but then the peppers hit, and before I know it, I'm coughing as tears stream from my eyes.

I rub at them, and although I'm able to staunch that flow, my nose starts running. Which means I have to run to the kitchen for something, anything, to stop the snotty pour. When I emerge, red-eyed, red-nosed, Colt has a nacho raised to his lips.

Maybe it's out of sympathy or maybe it's out of curiosity, but Colt takes a bite. His eyes watering, he chews and swallows quickly.

"They don't hold back with the seasoning," he says.

I wink. "That's an understatement."

"Have you ever suggested that they could back off a little?" He tentatively rubs his tongue along the roof of his mouth. "I think I lost a couple of tastebuds."

I shake my head. "I don't want to hurt their feelings. They try so hard."

For a long moment, Colt stares at me, his eyes unreadable, as the singer croons about *amor*. The air crackles around us.

Kiss me, I tell him in my head. *Let's forget this terrible night.*

Of course, in my head, I race ahead to the part where his lips come crashing down on mine in a kiss to rival all kisses, my earlier dreams of him coming true. I lean forward, eyes closed, lips puckered, but . . . nothing happens. Mortified, I pretend to cough again as my eyes pop open.

Colt is reaching for the remote.

He wants to watch television?

I give up on my aspirations of kissing him and flop back on the sofa. Fine. I'll veg out to some mindless reality television show.

The television snaps to life, the screen filling with the shooting. I shudder as I'm hurled back to bullets whistling near me, the terror-filled screams, the thunk of bodies hitting the pavement.

Then, I remember who I was going to talk to if Colt didn't work out—although I don't know if I'd call him pointing a gun at me working out.

Was Alexander okay?

On-screen, the newscaster starts talking as a box flashes on the bottom part of the screen. I read:

Actor Alexander Benoit has been identified as one of the victims in a mass shooting outside of an Austin, Texas, bar by an unidentified sixteen-year-old. In a terrible stroke of irony, he was on location filming a movie about one of the first mass shootings, which occurred at Stephen F. Austin High School. Unlike the character he was playing, Benoit is no longer with us.

8

I fall back into the chair. As I had before, I slide down its slippery fabric to end on the floor. This time, neither of us laughs. Instead, I curl myself into a tight ball and cry for everyone and everything, but most of all, for Alexander.

We might not have been great friends—like most super famous people, I doubt he had great friends—but, in a crazy, merciless world, we'd shared a few laughs, and that counts for something.

Alexander had so much to give, and now he would never have a chance to do so. Even his legacy as an actor would be slight since he'd been killed before he could sink his teeth into the meaty roles. When he was remembered, if he was remembered at all, it would be as a minor piece of trivia.

Why not me? I ask once again.

Being born into money sounds like the dream, but it also means finding a dream is a lot harder. Even if I do find a passion, buckle down and pursue it, maybe becoming successful, the whispers would follow me for the rest of my life. *It's because of her dad. It's because she bought her way in. It's because she started with every advantage possible in life.*

And no matter how false I proved the chatter, a grain of truth would always be present. Because I did start, will have always started, on third base. Pretending otherwise is offensive for those who start in the parking lot.

The tears drip down my cheeks until the well runs dry. My emotions, though, are still on fire as I start to relive the shooting. Seeking some type of exit, they push at my skin until I'm shaking. The convulsions are violent, like I'm having a seizure. Although I'm cold, sweat streams down my body, slicking my skin and making me even colder.

Before I even realize what's happening, Colt scoops me up.

"You're in shock," he says. "You need to lie down."

I'm too overcome to think straight. Instead, I stay coiled against him, pressing myself against his warmth, as he tries to enter the bathroom before figuring out which door is the one to my bedroom.

He places me gently on the bed. My dress rides up, bunching itself around my upper thighs. Colt pauses and then reaches up to pull it down. My skin feels seared by his touch, which is gentle yet authoritative.

"Sorry," he says. "No disrespect meant. I want you to be comfortable."

I open my mouth to say something, but nothing comes out. Or maybe I do say something, but my shaking covers it. I'm too out of it to stand outside myself and judge.

He doesn't notice. He's too busy walking around my bedroom, grabbing pillows from an armchair and a throw blanket off the bench. Colt slides the pillows under my legs and tucking a blanket around my convulsing form. He pivots my face ninety degrees, I assume, to keep me from choking if I vomit. Using his hand, he strokes my body, warming me up, from the outside in although it feels like the inside out, his hand stoking a fire deep inside me.

We stay like that for ages until the shaking subsides. I start to inhale deeper breaths. The shock has subsided although my emotions feel charred beyond belief.

"Did you know Alexander?" Colt asks.

I nod. "Not well, but we were friendly."

"How'd you meet?"

"An after-party. The Emmys, I think."

"The Emmys," Colt repeats. "You have some life."

I press my hands together. "The magazines and gossip blogs make it sound glamorous, but it's like going to the office holiday party except everyone just happens to be beautiful or rich. After you've been to one, you've been to them all."

He wrinkles his forehead. "Why go if you hate it so much?"

I throw my head back and exhale. How do I explain this world to someone who isn't part of it, who thinks it's as simple as staying home from the Emmys?

"When you're like my family," I say, "you don't have a lot of options as far as who you hang out with. Lots of people may pretend to be my friend, but they're really trying to scam me or use me." I shrug. "That leaves actors and rock stars for new friends since they know what it's like to live an abnormal life." I sigh. "At least they're different."

"So, you met Alexander there?"

I shrug. "We found ourselves out on a balcony at the same time, watching the sunset. It was gorgeous, like an Impressionist painting in gold, orange, and lilac. Alexander, though, seemed agitated. I said to him, 'You're a famous movie star, watching the sun set in New York, and you seem upset. Is the champagne not expensive enough for you? The caviar subpar?'"

I fiddle with the strap of my sundress. "My jokes were dumb, but I wanted to make him laugh. If a gorgeous movie star can't be happy, then who can?"

"Did he laugh?"

I shake my head. "So I asked him what was wrong."

"Did he tell you?"

"He didn't have to. I put my hand on his shoulder, and he flinched. That's when I knew the rumors that he was asexual were true."

"That's a problem?"

"If you're a famous actor, your job doesn't stop when the

cameras aren't rolling. You're supposed to maintain a visible presence, especially as a young, good-looking man."

"Doing what? Partying?"

"Yeah, but not in a drug-using, rehab-entering way. That's bad for business. But in a man-about-town way that sells magazines and newspapers."

Colt nods although his eyes narrow like he's putting puzzle pieces together.

"Anyway, I backed off, so he knew his secret was safe with me. We'd chat when we ran into each other at parties, and that was it." I look off into the distance, remembering the few times I'd bumped into him. "If it didn't work out with you, then I was going to try to say hi to him." I hesitate. "Nothing happened the way I thought it would."

9

Colt gives me a quick squeeze with one arm around my shoulders. Technically, it's nothing, the same thing anyone would do to someone else to show comfort. But there's something about the way his arm, warm and corded with muscles, that makes me feel like anything is possible, that I survived the shooting for a reason.

I glance at him, his blond hair swooping in his eyes, and my heart closes around the seed that was planted earlier. I let it sink down where, maybe, it will bloom, and I will give the world something.

Colt brings me a glass of iced water, which I sip. As the water flows through me, rational thought returns, which has nothing to do with that planted seed because, that's right, I'm here with a guy who has both pulled a gun on me. But why? He could have robbed or raped me, and all he's done is take care of me.

I want answers, so I ask him point-blank, "Why are you here?" I ask. "Why do you keep pulling a gun on me?" My voice raises. "I need to know."

"I can't answer either question."

"Then what's going on?" My voice is shrill.

"I can't tell you that."

"What can you tell me?" My pulse is starting to race, and I'm worried I might go into shock again if I get upset.

He sighs. "You're not in any danger."

"Really? Because you have a gun, and I have nothing."

He yanks out the gun tucked into his waistband and opens the chamber. The bullets tumble out, six soft clinks as they hit my bed. He gathers them up and tips his head at me.

"Hold out your hand."

Surprised, I extend my fingers without thinking. He dumps the bullets into my palm. I close my hand around them. The bullets are smooth and cool, smaller than I think they should be considered the damage they can do.

"I have a gun," he says. "You have the bullets. One without the other is useless."

"How do I know you're not lying?"

Colt pulls out his pockets inside out. A set of keys and a smartphone falls beside me. He reaches around to his back pocket and removes a wallet. From the other pocket, he places a handkerchief beside the other items. He slips his arms out of his denim jacket and hands it to me. "Check it out for yourself."

I paw through the pockets, trying and failing to ignore the warmth of his jacket, the way it smells of him—tawny but clean.

I hand it back to him. "Nothing." I open my hand and let what I did find drift beside his wallet and keys. "Except for some lint."

"You're thorough."

"I have to be. I don't know why you're here."

Colt sweeps his hand over it. "This is all I have on me."

"Are you going to leave now?"

He shakes his head. "I have to confirm your story."

"But you said you believed me."

"Just because I do doesn't mean the people I work for do." His nostrils flare as if he's annoyed, like he told me something he shouldn't.

I can't stop myself even though I know he won't give me an answer. "Who do you work for?"

He just laughs.

I flop on the bed and stare at the ceiling. My legs are hanging off the side of the bed, which has twisted my back into a contorted C. I want to throw my legs on the bed to even myself out, but Colt's jacket still rests at the end. Really, I should just lob my legs on top of it, seeing as he's invaded my home.

I don't. I'm still not sure why he's here, but I'm starting to think it's for an important reason.

As I stare at the ceiling, an idea forms. Maybe idea isn't the right word. Want is probably more accurate. I want to find out why Colt is here. Why does he have a work badge with the name Marvin Martins on it even though that's not his real name? Why did he follow me home?

I want to know who he works for, what he does, where he goes for work.

I want to know because, maybe, it might be something I'm interested in.

Although I don't know Colt that well, I've spent enough time with him to know that, while he might not tell me the truth, he acts honestly. I've passed plenty of hours around wealthy people and their hangers-on to recognize when someone is comfortable in their skin and confident about their choices in life.

Colt is that person. He's not the only person I've met like that, but he is the first in Texas. I wiggle in excitement. I'm going to find out what's going on and then see if I can insert myself into it.

I switch my gaze to Colt, who's looking at me.

You have no idea what's about to happen, I think as I smile innocently at him. *Once I decide I want something, I will stop at nothing to get it.*

I watch the digital clock beside my bed flip to the start of a new day. Colt is in the living room, his legs hanging over the armrest of the leopard print loveseat. I'm wide-awake in the bedroom, just waiting for him to give me a sign that he's asleep.

Before he closed my bedroom door behind him, he told me I should be cleared by morning. Which means I have seven to ten hours, depending on what he means by morning. Hopefully, he means after nine o'clock.

Regardless, I don't have much time to set my plan in action.

Step one: I'm going to find out as much as I can about Colt. Once I know that he's truly asleep, I'm going through his wallet and seeing if I can get into his cellphone.

How hard can it be? People do it all the time on television. I'll find out his birthday from his ID—the real one has to be in his wallet—and use it to unlock his phone. And if it's not his birthday, I'll look for other numbers like an address.

I practically quiver with pride at how great this plan is. I may be failing my junior year of college for the third time, but I've already figured out how to glean the basics from Colt.

I wait another fifteen minutes before shoving my feet into a pair of fluffy purple slippers. Although they're tacky, they should muffle the sound of my footsteps.

I mentally pat myself on the back for thinking ahead as I push open my bedroom door inch by inch. A gentle, steady wheeze greets me.

I sigh in relief. It's official; Colt is asleep. I tiptoe, barely breathing to the mirrored end table where his wallet and phone lay. I'm doing great until I trip over the edge of my fuchsia-fur rug. I try to swallow my instinctive curse, but I'm too late. It tumbles out of my mouth and echoes through the living room. I freeze.

In my head, I plan my defense. *I'm getting a glass of water, I'm looking for a book, I need to get the charger for my phone.*

I should have saved myself the effort. Colt doesn't move. I sidle over to the end table, snatch his wallet and phone, and then skitter back to the bedroom.

I sink onto my bed, breathing heavily, which is ridiculous, considering I maybe walked a couple of dozen steps back and forth. I open the wallet and dump out the contents.

There's not much: a few hundred dollars in small bills and a handful of identification cards. I place the cash off to the side and focus on the IDs. One by one, I turn them over and put them in a row. It only takes a couple before I figure it out.

They're all fakes. Some are work badges while others are driver's licenses. There's even a military one in the bunch. The same picture graces them all. Colt with his chin dipped and his blond hair falling over his left eye as if he forgot to look straight at the camera.

Or chose not to look at the camera.

The names and addresses are variations on the same theme: Peter Pritchens at 1616 Pond Lane, Wayne Winkler at 2323 Wind Court, Charles Coughlin at 3939 Cloud Street.

I scan them all, hoping to find a clue that will make help me make sense of who Colt really is. Besides the fact that all the addresses are based in Austin and have pictures of Colt, there's no unifying information like a birthdate or a height or even an eye color, with some having it as brown while others say hazel.

I throw my hands up in frustration. Colt remains a cipher.

I grab his phone and turn it on. Of course, it needs a passcode, which I haven't the foggiest idea of figuring out. And it doesn't have any type of identifying picture, just a screen saver that's a stock photo of falling snow. The screen is pristine with no grid of fingerprints that might help me figure out what his passcode is.

I groan. All my efforts and I'm still at zero. Plus, I still have to put everything back in the order I found it, which I don't remember because I was so excited that I didn't pay attention to how everything was organized.

In my head, I plan my story. *I went to grab my phone charger, and I bumped into the table. Your wallet fell—*

"Nice slippers." Colt is leaning against the doorjamb, his arms crossed. He nods at the spread of IDs in front of me, the phone clutched in my suddenly sweaty hand. "Find what you were looking for?"

10

Colt's phone slips from my hand as I grasp for something, anything that will explain that what I'm doing—going through his wallet and phone—is not at all what I'm actually doing.

Nothing comes to mind because, for real, there's no explanation. I was snooping, and I got caught red-handed. So I dive into honesty.

I meet Colt's eyes. He hasn't budged from the doorframe.

"I didn't find what I'm looking for. All I found were more questions."

"What kind of questions?"

"Who are you?" I frown. "Not your family name or where you're from, but why are pretending to be . . ." I pick up a driver's license. "Peter Pritchens?" I rub the license between my fingers. "I don't know you, but I suspect it's for a good reason."

Colt doesn't say anything for a long moment before he straightens up and strides to the bed. He picks up his phone and punches in a string of numbers, way more than the normal four digits I use for a passcode. He scrolls a few times and then stops, presumably to read an email or a text.

"Your story checks out." He tucks the phone into the pocket of his jeans. "Sorry for the inconvenience." He scoops up the IDs, tucks them into his wallet, and turns to leave.

I swing my legs off the bed and stand. "Wait."

He stops mid-stride, his eyes curious, his lips soft and parted. I catch up to him, trying to think of something to say that will keep him here, with me, until I can solve this mystery of a man. Nothing comes to mind, so I go with my gut, which has read his body language, and I do something so stupid it should be illegal.

I kiss him.

And in that kiss, I try to tell him why he should stay.

I fully expect Colt to pull away and then run away from clumsy, reckless me.

He doesn't, and for that, I will be forever grateful because this is a kiss for the memory bank. I throw my arms around him and press myself against his body. Colt responds by shifting himself forward until we bleed together like two watercolors dissolving into each other. His hot-silk tongue wraps around and caresses me. With a finger, he traces the contours of my earlobes as I shiver, having had no idea until this moment how sensitive that part of my body is.

As the kiss deepens, I give myself over to it. I follow his lead, let him take control, show me things.

If it were an option, I would have stayed like this forever, but Colt pulls away.

"Try to get to class, Libby. Write that paper."

"Don't." I step in front of him and spread my arms wide. "Please stay. I'll pay you."

He laughs. "I'm not a gigolo."

My cheeks feel like they've been singed. "I didn't mean it like that."

Although who am I kidding? I would love nothing more than to fall into bed with Colt and let him make me forget everything except how good it feels to be skin to skin with a gorgeous man.

"How did you mean it?"

I go for the truth, just not the whole truth. "I'm scared to be alone right now. I don't have any friends to call, and my parents are in Connecticut." I look down at my feet still clad in my fluffy slippers. I can only imagine how I look to Colt.

"I'm not stupid enough to think that you don't have places to be and important things to do," I say, still staring at my slippers. My right big toe is starting to poke a hole, my sparkly nail polish winking in the dim light. "So I'm offering to pay you."

"I don't need your money."

And, just like that, I've been made irrelevant. What most people don't know, mostly because they'll never get a chance to know, is that money can buy you almost everything—even happiness, and if not happiness, then something adjacent to it.

What it can't buy me is Colt.

I'm more disappointed than I should be. But something—call it intuition, call it a hunch—tells me that I need to stay close to Colt. That if I do, something wonderful and maybe a little weird will happen. That he might hold the key to kicking the funk I've been in for years.

I know one thing for sure. He stands that straight because he's proud of himself, and that incentivizes me to want to stand beside him.

But I literally have nothing else to offer beyond my money, so I try again, but in a different way. "Maybe you don't need the money, but I bet you know somebody who does. And even if they don't need it right now, they might need it in the future."

It's like I've spelled *BINGO*.

His eyes dart back and forth, and I can practically see his brain work through my offer.

Got you.

"How much money?" he asks.

I stand on tiptoe and whisper into his ear.

He exhales. "That's a fair amount." Colt's eyes narrow. "I thought you were living on your dad's dime. How are you going to assemble that much money?"

"I'm going to pretend to go to rehab," I say, the answer super obvious to me. "Everyone I know has been. My parents won't blink when I tell them I need the money for it."

"But wouldn't they just cut a check to whatever pretend rehab center you'll go to?"

I shake my head. "When I have an . . . unexpected expense, the accountant just deposits money in my account. He's busy enough as it is to write check after check for my mistakes."

"I take it you have a lot of unexpected expenses."

I flush. "Some." I hesitate and then straighten my shoulders. "But this is different. This is for something good." I look at him through my lashes. "I can't imagine you would give the money to someone who doesn't need it."

"You would imagine right." Colt gazes at me for an endless minute. "You have one chance to make this real."

"Okay," I say unsurely.

"I'm going to ask you one question, and if you answer it right, then we can hang out for a week, and you'll cut a check to the name I give you." He holds my gaze. "After that, we're done. You go back to school, and I go on my merry way."

I nod, wondering who Colt cares about so much to give that much money to. It must be someone important.

A girlfriend?

I throw that thought out, mainly because it's too depressing to entertain.

"I need you to say it out loud. Do you understand?"

"I do." I cross my fingers that I'll be able to answer his question.

"Why did I intentionally walk into a mass shooting?" he asks.

My mouth opens and closes soundlessly. Of course, I don't know why he did it. I was trying to find that out by going through his wallet.

"Think, Libby, think." Colt's voice has a pleading edge, like he wants me to answer the question correctly.

I close my eyes and go through the scenario.

Still nothing.

I keep my eyes closed and try again, this time going more

slowly, focusing on the details until I see it—his livid expression at the end of the shooting even as he extends his hand to me.

At the time, I'd been too traumatized to understand why he seemed so angry with me. Now, I get it, and I wish I hadn't.

"You were there to stop the shooting," I say. "And I messed it up." I hold my head in my hands. "Because I'm a stupid, shallow idiot."

"Right." Colt pauses. "And wrong."

I look up through my tears. "Which is which?"

"I was there to stop the shooting. But you didn't mess it up."

My mouth drops. "I didn't?"

He shakes his head. "I wasn't near enough to the front. Even if I'd gotten closer, I likely couldn't have killed the shooter without killing innocent people in the process. And I'm under strict orders not to kill anybody who isn't the target."

"So you're an . . ."

"Assassin." He pauses. "Still want my company?"

11

Colt and I are sitting across from each other at an all-night diner. Cups of coffee rest in front of us, and we've put in orders for scrambled eggs and toast with a side of bacon for him.

I suggested the diner after Colt dropped his bombshell. Actually, bombshell isn't the right word at all. Maybe barrage of heavy artillery fire would be correct. After staring at him dumbfounded for what had to be several minutes, I said the first thing that came into my head.

Which was, *do you feel like getting something to eat?*

I should probably have called the police or told him to leave, but I didn't. For no good reason, I want to see my commitment through. At least going out to eat will help me digest the news that the man I'm paying to spend the week with me is an assassin.

I swallow my coffee as my brain swirls around the word assassin. Over and over, I think it, assassin becoming assassinassassinassassinassassinassassin—just a bunch of white noise even though, at a gut level, I know what it means.

Colt kills people.

For money.

My taste in guys has never been the best, but even for me, this is a new low.

And yet . . . something tells me there's an excellent reason why he's an assassin. Society might not think it's moral, but he definitely does.

I always thought assassins were a trope of Hollywood movies and crime novels. They were older and grizzled, usually with a Russian or maybe an Italian accent. They were cold, ruthless, efficient killers whose only motivation was a fat stack of cash.

They weren't supposed to be like Colt, who's young and handsome, and isn't in it for the money since he turned down my initial offer.

I make up my mind. I've got a week. I'm going to find out why he's an assassin. My parents wouldn't like this one bit. They kept me on a tight leash for years, worried that someone would pry for sensitive information and then bribe my dad. But they're not here right now.

I drain my coffee as the waitress clomps over to us, a pot of coffee clutched in her hand. Diners are on point with the coffee. She splashes tar-colored liquid into our cups and promises that our orders will be out soon.

"I'm normally a skinny, two-and-a-half-shot, size-medium, mocha-latte-chino girl, but this is pretty good," I say.

"And here I thought you were half-caf, sugar-free, almond-milk latte served at 120 degrees." He mock shakes his head. "My mistake."

I shoot Colt a smile as I dump a container of half-and-half in the steaming coffee and then add one package of sugar.

"I don't know how to work a coffee pot. I have one of those fancy espresso machines, which has about a million and one buttons. The first time I tried to make a latte, I burned myself. The second time, I set off the smoke alarm, and I had to call the fire department because I couldn't get it to stop screeching. That was fun."

"Fun?"

"Yeah, it's a real comedy act when the fire department thinks it's a legitimate emergency and races over with two engines and a half dozen firefighters. When they showed up, I had a hammer in my hand. I was going so crazy from the noise that I was about to smash the smoke alarm to get it to stop." I laugh ruefully. "You can't imagine the talking-to the chief gave me. I felt like a naughty toddler."

I stir my coffee and look up through my eyelashes at Colt. He's staring at me, his expression unreadable.

"So that's why I'm happy with diner coffee," I say with a bright smile.

He doesn't say anything, just pours a container of half-and-half into his coffee. Still gazing at me, he rips open a pack of sugar and tips it in.

The assassin likes his coffee the same as me.

Internally, I shake my head. The events of the last twelve hours have been so incredible that it'll take a lifetime to process them.

The waitress plunks down our orders. The food—all runny eggs and limp toast—doesn't look great, but I don't care. I'm starving, so I slop ketchup all over my plate and eat. I love ketchup and would put it on top of anything, but don't, mostly because I don't want people to make fun of me.

"How's your ketchup with a side of eggs and toast?" Colt asks.

I flush. So much for not having people make fun of me.

"I'm teasing. The gods have nectar. Us mortals have ketchup." He takes the bottle and dumps it over his plate.

I laugh and lift the last forkful of my ketchup-covered eggs to my mouth.

"I guess you have a few questions for me," Colt says.

I swallow and blot my lips. "I do. Although I'm not sure where to start."

"I'll start for you."

"At the beginning?"

He shakes his head. "You don't need to know that."

"Then where?"

"Near the end."

I frown. "Oh." I'd been hoping to get all the juicy details of

Colt's past. Instead, it sounded like he was going to start with what happened yesterday, which I already know. He had short-rib tacos for lunch and a beer at five o'clock.

"I'm an assassin who tries to stop mass shootings before they happen."

"How do you do that?" I ask.

"My job is the easy one."

"I doubt that."

"It is. I shoot someone before they shoot other people."

I gasp and cover my heart with my hand, the fingers splayed, like I'm an opera singer. It's melodramatic, but it reflects how shocked I am.

"You shoot them before they can shoot other people?" I echo. "How do you know who—"

"To shoot? I'm given instructions."

"By whom?"

He laughs. "Whom. I don't think I've heard anyone use that in real life."

"I loved myself some Victorian novels when I was young."

"I can't tell you from whom," he winks at me, which makes my heart stutter, "but I can tell you that a group of billionaires formed a pact to fight evil in the world."

I open my mouth to ask the obvious question—is my dad one of them?

C olt holds up his hand.

"Your dad isn't a member of the Billionaire's Pact."

"You know who they are?"

He shakes his head. "Not a clue. We do everything online using code names."

"Like Peter Pritchens?"

"Try long strings of letters and numbers."

"And that's . . ."

"To protect our anonymity and keep everything top secret. The Pact does a lot of good in the world, but they do it illegally."

"Why?" I ask. "They could go to jail and lose all their money."

"That's not going to happen. You don't get to be a billionaire by being stupid or careless. They plot out every variable and know all the ways a job can go wrong before they assign it. They present it to us, the assassins, and we decide if we'll take it. If we say no, they ask for our reasoning and go back to the drawing board."

I stop to think about my dad and his approach to business. Instead of yes-men and yes-women, he likes no-men and no-women. "You can't win if you don't know how you can lose," he always says. He wants people to argue with him and point out all the way he could fail.

"What kind of work does the Pact do?" I ask.

"They kill criminals or those who are about to commit a crime."

"Aren't there better ways than . . . killing someone?"

"None that will stop evil in its tracks."

"So you kill people who are about to kill other people."

This morality is a Gordian knot, something so tight and twisted and intricate that I don't know how to unravel it.

He nods before putting his finger to his lips. The waitress is approaching, a coffee pot in her hand. I use the opportunity to jump up and run to the restroom. I need a moment away from the crazy conversation I'm having with Colt, who apparently assassinates people for good.

I lean my head against the mirror. The glass feels cool and clarifying against my heated skin. I stay for a few minutes before I pull back to study my reflection.

My strawberry blonde hair hangs limply around my face, and my smudge-proof mascara has failed to live up to its promise. It's drifted off my eyelashes to end in half-moons under my eyes, which now look like two big, blue bruises.

It's stupid to care about how I look considering everything that has happened and, maybe, everything that will happen. Even still, I fluff my hair and rub the dark dust from beneath my eyes. It's not much, but it will have to do for dinner with an assassin.

I head back to the table, still in my head. I stop a few steps away because, on our table, is a slice of lemon meringue pie. The flame from a single candle flickers in the breeze from the air conditioner because, even in April, Austin is as hot as a convection oven.

My birthday wish is coming true. I'm celebrating with Colt.

My eyes fill with tears, threatening to ruin all the good work I did in the bathroom. To hide my happy embarrassment, I slide into the booth and crack a joke.

"You don't think I've been through enough today? I need to be reminded that I'm a year older?"

"Technically, you're only a day older than you were yesterday."

He grins at me as my heart does a jig. "It just happens to be the one day a year that it counts. Happy Birthday."

"Thanks," I whisper, staring at the slice of pie. It feels like a sweet but literal arrow pointing to a new direction, which is to me, a new Libby.

Colt gestures to the pie. "You should blow that candle out. It's about to singe the meringue."

I blow harder than I need to, which dislodges the candle from its sticky, sugary base. I pick it up and lick the meringue from its bottom.

"I'm pleased to announce that this does not need ketchup." I wave the candle at Colt, who's gazing at me, his eyes warm.

Suddenly shy, I push a fork toward him. "Try it yourself."

We eat in companionable silence until crumbs dust the plate. The mood between us shifts, the joking around giving away to something more serious.

"What's next?" I ask, pushing the plate away.

"Do you still want to tag along?"

I nod. "I don't know how I'm going to be of any use to you or an assassination or the Pact . . ." I hesitate, the words feeling weird and heavy in my mouth. "But I'd like to do something. As long as it's not working a fancy coffee machine," I add to break the tension.

He lifts his hand for the check as his face hardens into seriousness. "Anything else beyond that?"

I think back through everything that's happened today. Whatever I thought was true isn't true anymore, and to act like I could state absolutes with certainty seems dumb. So I tell Colt the truth. "I don't know. I really, really don't. But when I do, I'll tell you."

"Works for me."

I twist my hands under the table. "What's next?"

Are we going to hit the road to intercept the next potential mass shooter? Stake out a potential criminal's home? Book plane tickets to do the first two?

"We're going to get some sleep. In the morning, we'll get the rehab story straight. Then, you're going to meet someone."

"Someone from the Pact?" My pulse starts to race. Will I recognize, maybe even know, this billionaire? It's not like our crowd is robust in size.

Colt shakes his head. "Someone even more important."

13

I don't know what to expect when Colt pulls up to a boring, beige apartment complex in Round Rock, which is north of Austin. No billionaire lives here, that's for sure.

It was a weird drive, with Colt looking in the rearview mirror every minute or so. He even drove around the same block twice as if he were shaking a tail. He started freaking me out, so I started looking too. At one point, I could have sworn I saw X and O in a car behind us, their mouths moving at the same time.

But I shook that off, sure I was wrong. Why would X and O be following us?

"Did you lose whoever was following us?" I ask. "Perhaps it was the dream team of Xaviera and Orpita, staking out our every move."

He ignores the questions as my mind cycles through the options of who we're here to see and who we lost on the way. Is it another assassin? A double agent? I land on the unpleasant thought I had earlier. A girlfriend?

Nothing that's happened between us has suggested Colt has a girlfriend. Or even a family for the matter. After our middle-of-the-night breakfast, we headed back to my apartment where we slept together. Which is to say we slept in my bed, him on one side, me on the other, our fingers loosely interlaced.

I couldn't fall asleep, my every nerve on high alert with Colt so close. His tawny scent wafted over me, and I took small sniffs every now and again until he asked if I needed a tissue. Embarrassed, I closed my eyes and forced my mind still as he took my hand in his. Using his index finger, he stroked the outline of each of my nails until I fell asleep. He shook me awake in what felt like minutes, but was, in fact, hours.

I made a quick call to my mom, who still seems shaken that I was at the shooting. She accepted my off-the-cuff story about how I hadn't done anything except go to class and study, which made me depressed, and I self-medicated with wine. *I'm worried that my drinking is going to get out of hand now that I have images of the shooting to keep me up at night* is what I told her.

"At least you'll be safe there," my mom said. "You sure your professors will let you hand in your assignments?"

I assured her that they would although I had no intention of asking that, and she agreed to have the accountant add money to my bank account.

Now, it's high noon. We've parked the Barbie-mobile and are striding through a lobby that's decorated in different, but still depressing shades of beige. As we turn down a hallway, Colt stops.

"You don't have to say anything," he says. "But what you do say needs to be nice."

I blink. Why would he think I would be anything but nice? Baffled, I trail behind Colt as he thumps on the door.

"Bro Bro," a voice says as the door swings open.

"Bri Bri," Colt responds in a sweet tone.

I peek over his shoulder. A man—younger than Colt but with the same blond hair—has his arms held out. It must be his brother, but something in his appearance doesn't jibe with Colt's.

Then, the brother steps back. He's short and a little pudgy, but it's the shape of his eyes that makes me understand Colt's warning. His brother has Down's Syndrome.

He points at me. "Who's that?"

"This is Libby."

I slip past Colt and smile. "What's your name?"

"Brian. But you can call me Bri Bri like my brother."

"Nice to meet you, Bri Bri." I step into the apartment, taking in Brian, who is well-groomed with his shoelaces tied in pert bows and his hair neatly parted and wetted down. Frantically, I try to think of something to say, but I'm not sure what to say beyond "how are you," which I say fast and in an ultra-high voice.

If I do a terrible job of putting Brian at ease, then Brian does a great job of putting me at ease. He latches on to my question.

"I'm great, " Brian says. "Today is Wednesday, so it's laundry day. I'm folding in the kitchen. Come see." He takes me by the hand and tows me into a little nook where a pile of clothing rests on a small dining table. "I just finished pants."

"Can I help?" I ask.

He frowns. "I always do socks next."

"I could . . ." I trail off as, internally, I curse myself. Besides knowing that Down's Syndrome exists, I know nothing about it. Brian is still frowning as if he's trying to figure out how to deal with my offer. I decide that maybe I should let Brian continue with his routine, and I'll take my cues off him.

"I have an idea," I say. "Will you show me how to fold socks? I keep shoving one of them into the other and then balling them up. My socks seem pretty upset about that treatment, seeing as about half of them have disappeared."

Brian nods as he grabs a pair of white tube socks. He stretches them out on the table until there are no wrinkles or bunches. Then he places one sock on top of the other. Slowly, carefully, he rolls the pair until it's a neat cylinder. He repeats the task until a half-dozen or so pairs stand in a neat line.

"You did a great job!" I say. I'm telling the truth too. Brian's socks look like foot soldiers ready to march off to war.

Brian doesn't even so much as look up to acknowledge my praise. "I know."

Colt catches my eye and winks. "Brian is one of the most honest people you'll ever meet."

"I am," Brian says as he reaches for a pile of T-shirts.

For the next half hour, I watch Brian fold clothes, picking up tips about how to properly tuck a T-shirt into a perfect square. After seeing him in action, I have a new appreciation for the geometry of folding clothes. He's a mathematician who creates hard planes from the soft folds of clothes.

Colt hangs back, watching me watching Brian. I smile at Colt a couple of times, which he returns with a slight upturn of his lips. I want him to know that I like Brian, that I'm glad to be here.

"All done," Brian says. His clothes look like they've come out of their packaging—that's how precise the creases and folds are. He takes a handful of T-shirts in his hands. "Time to put away."

"I'll help," I say. I pick up a couple of pairs of socks in one hand and then grab the rest with my other hand. I turn to follow Brian, but I'm not paying attention, and I trip over the chair leg.

I have to make a quick decision. I can throw Brian's socks on the floor and grab the table to steady myself. Or I can hold on to the socks and fall.

I keep hold of the socks.

I hurtle to the floor, landing on my butt, the socks clutched to my chest.

I scramble to my feet. "I'm fine." I lift the socks overhead in a victory salute. "And I saved the socks."

Brian is laughing as is Colt.

"You looked so silly," Brian says. "Falling on your butt like that."

I toss my hair. "That wasn't even my best move. You should see the one where I logroll off a chair."

Colt says, "I've seen that one. It's a stunner."

I mock frown at Colt as we follow Brian down the tiny hall to his bedroom.

"You'll be writing the check to Brian," he says in a quiet tone. "It'll go into a trust to keep him in a place like this where he lives in his own apartment but with around-the-clock supervision." He meets my eyes. "Just so you know."

"It'll be the best money I've ever spent," I say. "That's the truth, too."

And it is the truth. It's buying me Colt for a week and Brian's care for a nice long while.

Colt pulls me close and presses his lips against mine. It's a quick, rough kiss, but I don't care because I know what he's trying to tell me in it.

I startle and almost drop the socks for the second time until—

Buzz. Buzz. Buzz.

The buzzing is insistent, and it's coming from Colt's pocket. He reaches for it, his expression changing from tender to fierce in the second it takes to read the message. His voice, though, doesn't change as he addresses Brian. "Bri Bri, it's almost time for you to do puzzles with your friends in the common room. Libby and I have to say goodbye."

Brian turns around. "Will you come back next week? It was fun to fold laundry with you."

"I had fun, too. And I'll be back. Maybe next time, you can teach me how to make a bed with hospital corners. That's another thing I'm terrible at." I'm lying through my teeth since, by next week, I'll have written my check for my time with Colt.

My shoulders droop. I've enjoyed the easy banter among us, the way I always imagined it would be in a small-but-close family with siblings or cousins my own age.

"You're terrible at lots of things," Brian says with no malice.

"I am." I glance at Colt. "Fortunately, your brother thinks I have some raw talent that can be developed under his supervision."

Brian gives me a big hug, which makes me feel squishy on the inside. When he lets go, I say, "my turn," and hug him.

"Libby." Colt's voice has a dark, pleading edge to it. "We have to go."

"I'll see you soon, Bri Bri," I say.

Colt pulls me to the door as I wave over my shoulder at Brian.

"What's going on?" I ask. "I thought we were having fun."

He doesn't slow his stride. "There's another shooter. I have to stop him, and I need your help."

14

I n a daze, I follow Colt to the Barbie-mobile. He doesn't seem to notice my dumbfounded state. He's looking around him, checking out the parking lot. He nods in a satisfied way as he starts the car.

Mechanically, I buckle my seatbelt, turning over Colt's words: *I have to stop him, and I need your help.*

So *we* are going to do this together. As in the two of us. But for all my big talk yesterday, I have no idea how I'm going to help Colt, much less stop a shooter.

I gaze out the window. Although the bluebells are in season, blanketing the meridian between the highways with undulating indigo and purple blossoms, I'm too amped up to appreciate the beauty, which is like Texas itself—supersized and showy.

It takes a couple of miles before I realize where we're going—the place I should have been yesterday—the University of Texas. On the bright side, I'm putting in an appearance today although I won't be attending my Politics through Film class.

"How are we going to know who it is?" I rub my hands together. "The shooter, I mean."

"I know."

"Are you going to tell me?"

He shakes his head.

"Why, then, am I with you?"

"To call the police if I can't stop him."

"Stop him?" I ask incredulously. "Are you going to kill him?"

"Yes."

"Why not call the police and give them an anonymous tip?"

"By the time the police get there, he'll be done."

"Aren't there police on campus?"

He throws me a withering look. "There are armed security guards."

"Isn't that the same thing?"

"Try again."

I throw my hands in the air. "They both have guns. What's the difference?"

"Training and experience."

I think for a minute. "It's Texas. Everybody carries a gun. Why not let one of the many, many people packing heat stop the shooter?"

Colt brakes at a stoplight and turns to face me. His brownish-gold eyes look like marbles, that's how hard they are. "This is my job, Libby. I stop the bad guy before he can pump bullets into the good guys."

"I know," I say in a small voice.

He laughs without humor. "Still happy you're spending the week with me?"

I don't answer Colt's question.

"I know you, like everyone else, think that gunfights in real life should be like the movies, but do you think a couple of scared kids leaving Comp Lit are going to be able to take down a mass shooter?"

"Maybe?"

He jerks the car into drive as the light turns green. "It only works like that in the movies. Do you know why?"

I shake my head.

"Because in the movie everybody has choreography. They

know the marks they're supposed to hit and the times when they're supposed to shoot. In real life, only the shooter has choreography. Everyone else is reacting. And even if someone is able to react with their gun, how well do you think they're going to do?" He doesn't wait for me to answer. "Not great. It's why none of these mass shootings have Hollywood endings."

"How do you normally stop them?"

He sighs. "That's been the problem. I haven't been able to stop them."

I shudder, remembering last night.

"Is it me, or are there more shootings than there used to be?"

"You would be right." Colt's jaw clenched. "These ones, though, aren't disaffected guys upset about girls ignoring them or white supremacists who're mad that we left the antebellum era long ago. These guys are trained for a purpose."

"Trained for a purpose?" I repeat.

He nods. "To shoot as many people as possible as precisely as possible." He pauses. "They're pretty good at it."

"How did you normally stop them?"

He laughs without humor. "I make it look like they committed suicide."

"Suicide?"

"Most of these guys are angry and isolated. It's not a stretch to believe they'd take their own lives."

"You've never had a problem?"

"Not a one. The Pact does their research. They send me the job, and I execute it."

"What changed?" I ask.

His forehead wrinkles. "That's what I'm trying to figure out." Colt tips his head back and forth as if he's deciding to tell me something.

"Tell me," I say. "Sometimes, a fresh set of ears can hear the problem in a new way." I shrug. "Anyway, since I'm here, you might as well make use of me. You already know I'm crap at folding socks and making coffee. Although," I wink, "once Brian teaches me to make hospital corners, watch out world."

"I've never met anyone like you, Libby. Funny, pretty, and game for anything."

"I'm rich, too. I've been told that's one of my best qualities." I go for lightness, but what pokes through the words is the truth I believe with all my heart: The only reason a man would want me is because I can buy him his heart's desire.

"That wouldn't even make the top ten reasons for me."

Although Colt keeps his eyes on the road, he places his hand on my thigh. Beneath his warm palm, my skin prickles. The effect he has on me is unsettling. I kissed a rock star on my eighteenth birthday, but it pales in consideration now. Colt is a revelation.

He rubs my leg as my breath sticks in my throat. "I doubt it would even make my top one hundred."

"Really? What reason could push being rich out of the top one hundred? That my big toe is longer than my second one?" My voice has a plaintive edge to it although I'm trying to be funny. I don't want him to know that I care—more than I should—about his answer.

"You have nice ears," he says.

"Oh." I look down, avoiding Colt's eyes. I don't want him to see my disappointment. I'd been hoping for something poetic, not nice ears, which sounds like something you'd say to a homely child.

"They look like two shells."

I perk up. While not exactly poetic, I can work with having ears like shells.

"Plus, they work pretty good."

"They work . . ." I flush as I get it. "I'm a good listener."

He nods. "You can't imagine how rare a quality that is. Speaking of which—"

Colt is about to tell me something deadly serious, so I brace myself as all our earlier humor evaporates. The swings in our conversation should give me whiplash, but instead, I feel more alive than I've felt in years.

"What changed in the shootings?" I ask, matching his grim tone. "And how long ago did it change?"

"It used to be the Pact was pretty good at identifying potential mass shooters. They employ people who impersonate angry young men online. These guys have forums and websites they like to hang out on."

"What kind of forums and websites?"

"The kind where people go to say the foulest things they can think of because they can stay anonymous. They all have their own slant. Some are anti-Semitic while others celebrate white supremacy. Lots are devoted to bashing women."

"Sounds like exactly the place where the best of the best losers hang out."

"Most of these guys are there to blow off steam. They talk a big game and then go play video games in their parents' basement."

"How do you find the bad guys?" I ask.

"The guys comb through the profiles, looking for signs. To be more specific, they look for the people who escalate their hatred."

"For instance . . ."

"Take someone who hates women. First, this guy will say a lot of nasty things. Then, he'll start talking about wanting to kill women as revenge for rejecting him. At this point, one of our guys will strike up a friendship with the potential killer. Our guy will present himself as a sympathetic listener and probe to see if he's serious." He shrugs. "99% of these people turn out to be nothing more than cranks."

"How do you identify the 1%?"

"We look for certain behaviors, like buying a lot of guns in a short period of time or laying out plans in private chatrooms. Once there are signs that the guy is serious, the Pact's hackers get into their computers. They check the browsing history and search their documents."

"What are they looking for?"

"Evidence. Has this person committed a plan to paper that gains in intricacy? Has he written a manifesto? Has he visited the website of a yoga studio or a hair salon—places where women congregate—a bunch of times? Has he spent time researching other mass—"

I interrupt. "But someone could do all those things and still not be a killer."

"I know that as does the Pact, which is why we wait and wait before taking action."

"What do you wait for?"

"The fuse to blow."

"The fuse to blow," I repeat slowly.

Colt nods. "It can take time, years even, but most of these guys get madder and madder. Minor slights, like a female server not refilling their coffee, become huge to them. Their rants online get weirder and wilder, and they start acting crazy except when they're working on their plan. That's where they stay cold and logical."

"Even still. How do you know?"

"When the Pact thinks they have a good target, they put an agent on his tail."

"They have a lot of resources," I say. "So many people, doing so many things, and none of you know each other."

He nods. "It's why they're successful."

"So what does the agent do?"

"He combs the target's residence, follows him through his daily routine, and bugs his phone."

"Aren't all of those illegal?"

"If we used legal methods, then we would never catch anybody."

"When do you go in for the . . ." I gulp. I'm still not exactly comfortable with the fact that the guy who makes my heart backflip is an assassin. "Kill," I finish in a low voice.

"Not until he's minutes away from shooting people."

Colt anticipates my questions. "The agent calls me when the target is close to acting. I stay in the vicinity and keep a low profile until the target gathers his guns. I shoot him right before he leaves.

Then, I stage it as a suicide."

"That's a complicated process," I say.

"It has to be. I'm killing someone. If I'm going to do that, then we all need to be sure that taking this one life ensures a lot more lives get to be lived."

"So what changed?"

"I've killed nine men before they could kill ten times that. But I've failed the last two times." His voice takes on a frustrated edge. "So have the other teams."

"The two times were last night and . . ."

"A couple of weeks ago in Phoenix." Colt's face droops as he turns the corner.

I shiver, suddenly cold. "I remember Phoenix. It was a movie theater filled with kids for a new flick about talking pets."

Tears spring into my eyes. Having lived through one myself, I know how terrifying it must have been, and that no one who was there will ever be the same.

"What happened in Phoenix?"

"The shooting happened with no warning—no mass buying of an arsenal, no disaffected person mouthing off on forums, no hint of anything, which meant I did nothing."

"They caught the guy, right?"

He nods. "He has no footprint on the internet beyond email and a few barely used social media accounts. He was a kid of fifteen, so he didn't have a bank account, which means someone supplied him with the guns. The Pact's hackers can't find much beyond the boy disappeared a couple of months ago. His home life was so broken it took weeks before a sharp-eyed teacher noticed he'd been absent and reported it." Colt's face grows tight. "The hackers can't fill in the blank spot, and the boy won't provide details beyond saying a snake ordered him to do it."

I wrinkle my brow. "A snake?"

"Makes no sense to me either."

I fall still and silent as we approach the Main Building. With its 307-feet tall clock tower, it was where, in 1966, Charles Whitman killed over a dozen people, injured more, and traumatized countless others.

"We're here," he says as he swings into an entrance. The pale buildings with their dark red roofs loom ominously.

"Colt?" My hands are clammy, and my skin has been dampened by a cold sweat. "What's the plan with this target? The nuts and bolts of what you're going to do?"

"Don't have a plan. Don't need one." His backbone is rigid. "I'll do whatever it takes to stop him."

There are so many things wrong with this non-plan that I stop breathing. He could be hauled off to prison. He could be wounded. He could even die. Every scenario I play in my head ends terribly.

But I'm not going to let any of them happen.

I cy sweat drips down my back as my brain sounds alarms. The only voice that comes through loud and clear is my heart, which lays out the situation for me: I have to stop Colt from stopping the shooter.

I can pretend I want to do this for virtuous reasons. That I want a chance to pay back the fact that I've escaped one mass shooting and save someone in return. That Colt has a baby brother who needs him, and I have nobody who needs me. *That, that, that . .* .

But there is only one *that*, and it's sitting beside me. I want to do it because I am falling for Colt—in a way I've never fallen for anyone. In all honesty, let myself fall for anyone.

And that's a huge, almost impossible problem because I am going to get my heart broken. In a week, I'll write him a check, and we'll both go back to our lives. But it's not at all what I want. I want him to stay with me or me to stay with him, which means I need to give him a reason to like me beyond the check I'm going to write.

He took me to meet Brian, so I could see firsthand that he plans to do something honorable with the money. Then, when it came time for me to pay up, I won't balk. But once I sign the check, it'll be *thank you, ma'am*, and I'll never see him again.

For me to have any chance with Colt, I need to show him not just who I am, but who I can be. So, even though I—just like Colt—have no plan, I've decided I'm going to stop the mass shooting.

Not that I have any idea how to do that.

So, thinking, I look out the window. It's early afternoon, which means classes are getting out. Some people are walking in clumps, chatting among themselves about this or that professor, this or that paper. Others are alone, their spines bent with purpose as they head to the library or another class. Many are talking on their phones.

Regardless of what they're doing, they're all doing it with a clear motivation. They know what they're doing, where they're going, and why they're doing all of the above. Although I don't know most of these people, I do know who they are—college kids.

That makes it easy to spot the person who doesn't belong. He's too young to be on campus. Even though UT has its share of young, smart kids, they all present the same—earnest and energetic, like puppies eager to do tricks for treats.

This kid has none of those qualities. He looks like he wandered onto campus by accident, his eyes wide and searching. He has no books, no sheaf of papers fluttering in the breeze, and no idea where he's going. He keeps looking at his phone and then up as if he's got a map but can't figure out how his real surroundings coordinate with the digital ones. Most of all, he looks scared, his oversized Astros jersey dwarfing his hunched shoulders and dropped head.

He's also has a duffel bag slung over a shoulder that bulges and pokes out in places. I might be new to the game, but I can guess what's in there—a whole bunch of guns.

I glance over at Colt, who hasn't seen the guy yet. He's too busy waiting for a gaggle of sorority girls to pass, his golden brows knitted together in frustration.

The opportunity is ripe for my taking.

"Gotta pee," I say with a big smile as I unbuckle my seatbelt. "Back in a sec." I jump out of the car before Colt can say anything.

I dash as fast as I can to where the boy is. I would be faster, but I chose another pair of high-heeled sandals this morning. I'd felt so proud of the chunky heels that topped out at two-and-a-half inches. I'd been sure to pair them with a short skirt, hoping to impress the man who'd spent the night in my bed but who'd done nothing more than hold my hand.

And yet, they are still ridiculous, which, by association, makes me ridiculous. I can't run—the heels are too wobbly, and my skirt keeps kicking up in the wind. The best I can is jog, one hand pushing down my skirt in an attempt to keep it from flashing my lacy panties to the world. I'm sure I look silly, but I don't care. I've got more important things on my mind, like the boy, who suddenly seems to know where he's going. He shoves his phone into his back pocket and takes off.

16

I curse under my breath as he disappears into a clump of kids heading toward the baseball diamond. I catch sight of his small body and bulky duffel bag before the tide of students obscures him again.

Then, I see his Astros jersey fluttering around him like a flag. With an annoyed gesture, he yanks the too-big neckline up. I haven't been in Texas all that long, but I have learned that sports are practically a religion here. No self-respecting Astros fan wears a jersey that is treated with that type of disrespect.

Not that it matters now.

Because I know where he's going, and I know what he's going to do.

A game is scheduled for today against LSU, which is why everyone is headed to the UFCU Disch–Falk Field. Baseball might be second to football in Texas, but on a sunny, temperate day like this, nothing beats watching a game while drinking beer that's been smuggled in.

I shudder. Longhorns fans will literally be sitting ducks for him.

I glance over my shoulder to see where Colt is before wishing I hadn't. He's abandoned the Barbie-mobile and is striding to me, his expression livid.

Go time, Libby, I say to myself. *Think of something. NOW.*

As my heart thumps against my chest, my brain snags on the corner of an idea. I'm going to recreate the scenario I experienced with Colt on Sixth Street. If I distracted Colt enough to interrupt his plans to stop a mass shooting, maybe I can do the same thing here.

I double my pace. In less than a minute, I've pulled astride with the boy, who doesn't notice me. I open my mouth to say something, but someone bumps into me. I trip into the boy. To break my fall, I grab onto his Astros jersey, which, fortunately, is made of a sturdy material that allows me to pull myself to standing.

"Oh my god," I screech. "I'm so glad I bumped into you, like literally, totally bumped into you." I giggle maniacally.

I've pitched my voice several notches higher than my normal one and turned my vocabulary into that of a breathless, overwhelmed freshman.

The boy turns to face me, his eyebrows arched in surprise.

"You weren't in class today, but Dr. Kilgore . . . ugh, he's such a pill; it's like he's never met a paper he didn't want to assign . . . anyway, he selected us to be partners for the debate."

"Excuse me," the boy says. Up close, he looks to be all of fifteen, his skin hairless and dotted with clusters of pimples.

"No, excuse me." I bat my lashes extra hard. "I was the one who bumped into you."

He turns to go, but I place my hand on his shoulder. Maybe it's because I'm the first girl to touch his fifteen-year-old self or maybe it's because he's gone a long time without being touched, but tears spring into his eyes.

That's all the cue I need.

I toss my arms around the boy's shoulder. "So what I was trying to tell you is that we were assigned to be partners in Western Civ, and we need to talk about our project. Which group affected

British history more: the Normans or the Angles? You'll argue one side, and I'll argue the other."

His eyes are wide, his jaw slack. He has no idea what I'm talking about because, duh, none of this is true.

I take advantage of his confusion and march him to a building filled with classrooms where, if my luck holds, I'm bound to find an empty one.

"Let's find an empty classroom and make a plan for our debate. You look like you could have been named Norman, so maybe you should argue for the Normans."

As I continue to babble, tugging the boy with me, a tawny scent hits my nose. Colt is close. I stop talking for a moment to organize my thoughts. I have to show him that I've got the situation under control.

I mock-widen my eyes. "That looks so heavy," I say, pointing at the duffel bag. "Maybe I could help you carry it?"

This is absolutely the wrong thing to say because it reminds it reminds the boy of what he is here to do.

He tries to pull away from me, but I tighten my grip on him.

"If you're going to the game, you might as well talk about our project. The LSU team is stuck in traffic, so they've delayed the start time by thirty minutes." I smile big at him. "Take a load off."

"I can't," he says although he doesn't move to go. "I need to stay out here."

At that moment, I get it. He's scared, and he doesn't want to do it.

Someone is making him do this, I think.

At that moment, Colt pulls up alongside us. In the space of a heartbeat, I pull the bag from the boy's shoulder and pass it to Colt.

The boy is so surprised that he just stands there, his mouth flapping open. "Give it back." His words, though, are empty, unconvincing.

"I'm sorry," I say, explaining myself to both Colt and the boy. "I had to."

The reality hits the boy, and he takes off. Although he's small, he's quick, and he might have gotten away save for his baggy Astros shirt. I grab a corner of the hem, which is all the time Colt needs. He tugs the boy in a half hug and drags him into a classroom.

I follow, closing the door behind us.

17

The late afternoon sun streams through the windows. The building is devoid of people, everyone at the baseball game or gone for the day.

The boy and I sit behind desks as Colt stands in front of us. Although he has his gun trained on the boy, I'm on high alert. Colt looks ferocious, his brows drawn and his lips pressed in a flat line. I shiver. He is an assassin. Will I have to see him performing his job?

I hope not.

"This can be easy, or this can be hard," Colt says. "Your choice."

Next to me, the boy is shaking. He's trying to be a man, though, so he squares his shoulders and meets Colt's gaze.

"You don't have to say anything. Nod yes or shake your head no."

The boy nods.

"Do you go to school here?"

He shakes his head.

Colt jerks a finger over his shoulder. "Do you have guns and ammunition in here?"

On the professor's desk lays the duffel bag. It seems like a risky place to park the bag, but few options present themselves in the wide-open classroom where not much lives beyond desks and a video screen.

The boy doesn't say or do anything. Colt shakes his gun at him. Finally, the boy nods.

"Were you going to shoot people with them?"

He nods again.

"Do you have an accomplice?"

The boy frowns, unsure.

"A friend or helper," Colt explains.

He shakes his head and, for the first time since we've entered the classroom, speaks. "I was supposed to do it alone. Everything from parking the car to pulling the trigger."

He has an accent, one I didn't notice outside with my heart pounding in my ears. It's not a Texas twang, though, where the vowels are stretched out like a string of bubblegum.

This is a blue-collar Boston accent. I know because the boarding school I went to for high school was in a suburb outside of Boston, and I heard this accent every time I ventured beyond the hallowed stone-and-ivy walls of the campus.

How did a kid from Boston end up in Austin to shoot up a baseball game?

Colt seems to have the same thought. "Sounds like you're a long way from home," he says, his voice softening a little.

The boy nods.

I turn to him conspiratorially. "Boston, I'd guess. It must hurt your heart to wear an Astros jersey."

He thumps his heart. "Red Sox fan till I die." Then he stiffens as he remembers what he was here to do, how it was going to end for him.

Colt leans forward. "I can promise you one thing. You're not going to die unless you do something stupid." With his thumb, he strokes the bullet chamber of his gun.

I tense as I remember Colt saying something similar to me. For as much as I've grasped analytically that he's an assassin who prevents mass shootings, I still can't emotionally process that his work involves a gun.

Next to me, the boy starts to shake.

This needs a woman's touch.

I catch Colt's eye. *My turn*, I mouth before turning to the boy.

"I feel like we got off on the wrong foot," I say with a big smile. "Specifically, my wrong foot. Sorry about bumping into you."

"No hard feelings."

No hahd feelings, I repeat to myself.

"Anyway," I continue, "you know why I did it, right? I couldn't let you shoot a bunch of my classmates."

He ducks his head, his cheeks reddening.

"I don't think you wanted to do it either," I say. "Am I right?"

"I . . ." He looks down at the desk. He grazes his fingers across the surface. "I wasn't going to do anything."

"Really?" I ask.

"Really."

"Then why were you strolling around campus with an arsenal of guns."

He presses his lips in a tight line. "I can't say."

A lightbulb flickers in the recesses of my brain. "Were you coerced?"

"I don't know what that means."

"It means forced to do something against your will."

"Maybe." He looks away from us both toward the window and then the door.

I switch tracks. My questions are spooking him, and he's going to bolt sooner rather than later.

"What's your name?"

"I can't tell you that."

I remember how coming up with the nickname of Colt for not-Marvin Martins helped him warm up to me. Maybe that'll work here. I think, taking in the boy's youth and Red Sox fandom. "Can I call you Babe? Like Babe Ruth."

His face brightens. "Sure."

Although this skinny kid has nothing in common with the legendary slugger, it still suits him. With his skinny limbs and wide eyes, he looks like a literal babe in the woods.

"How did you get from Boston to Austin?" I ask. "Seems like you're going backward through the alphabet."

"I came down with some other guys."

"Because you wanted to?"

Babe nods. "In the beginning. I'd been suspended from school for fighting a guy who was picking on my sister. A man found me one day when I was hanging outside a convenience store."

Colt adjusts his gun, so it's pointing away from Babe, who visibly relaxes.

"What did he tell you?"

"He said he was a representative from a school in New Mexico, outside of Albuquerque. A billionaire founded it for boys like me, who weren't doing well in school." He shrugs. "He had all kinds of pamphlets. They showed boys outside, playing baseball and planting gardens. There were animals and a bunch of arcade games. The man said that the students worked the land in the morning, did lessons in the afternoon, and spent the evening goofing off. After living in a crappy apartment in a dirty city, I thought it sounded great. The best of all, it was free." He smiles wistfully. "I begged my mom to sign the forms before getting on a bus. I couldn't wait to get there."

"I'm guessing that when you got there, you couldn't wait to get out of there."

"It was all fake. The pictures, the buildings, even the schedule were all made up."

"What was the reality?"

"It was a compound that trained us to be mass shooters."

My jaw drops. "A compound that trained you to be mass shooters?" I squeak.

Babe nods.

This may be the craziest thing I've heard of, and I'm falling for a guy who's an assassin.

My thoughts are racing, but I calm them and focus on Babe. Now is not the time to get freaked out by his revelation. So I tilt my body to him and put on my best listening face. He's speaking so low that I can hardly hear him.

"They trained us from morning to night. I would have run away, but the compound was in the middle of the desert, and I didn't know which way to go. I was worried that I'd die before I found people."

He shakes his head in disbelief. "The only thing I knew was that a billionaire funded the joint. Not that you'd know it from how terrible the place was. We ate runny oatmeal for breakfast and peanut butter sandwiches for lunch and dinner. I ate better in Boston when we were on food stamps," he finishes up furiously.

I glance at Colt, who doesn't look surprised, which surprises me. Because this is some new level of insanity that I can barely hold it in my head.

I shrug off Colt's placidity. Maybe assassins are trained not to betray their thoughts.

He nods at me to continue talking to Babe.

"So this man tricked you into becoming a mass shooter?" I asked. "Other kids too?"

"Yeah."

"How did they incentivize . . ." I stop myself, trying to think of a better word. "Convince you to do what they said beyond all the guns pointing at you."

"They threatened our families. I got a kid sister who's the only good thing my pops ever made before he left. The ba*stahd* . . ." His face scrunches up in hatred. "The guy who was in charge made me watch a video of her jumping rope and singing to her babydoll. On-screen, she told me she loved me and she hoped I would be home soon because she missed me." He clenches his jaw. "The ba*stahd* said her life was my payment if I didn't go through with it." He drops his head to hands before looking at me through his fingers. "What was I supposed to do?"

"Out of curiosity, who was this guy?" I ask.

"He told us he used to be a sharpshooter with the Army, and every once in a while, he'd make some poor kid who'd had a bad day at the range stand with an apple on his head. The bas*tahd* would shoot it off as a warning to the rest of us."

"Any distinguishing features?"

"He's small and thin, like a wire, with a tattoo of a hissing snake that went up his forearm." He thinks for a minute. "That probably describes lots of bad guys." His eyes brighten. "He had one foot that turned in. When he got surprised, he'd trip himself up. We couldn't laugh although it was funny, this scary guy who couldn't walk right."

"Sounds like he's a charmer."

Babe laughs without humor. "A charm*ah*. Yeah, that's what he is."

"Were there any other charmers there?"

"There were other guys who kept guns pointed at us and a dude who cooked, but they didn't have any power. Only the charm*ah* gave orders, and everyone jumped."

I think for a moment. I need more information, but the kid doesn't seem to have much.

"Do you know the name of the billionaire who funded it?" I ask, buying time as I try to think of better questions.

"Nope. The charm*ah* knew because he was taking care of the books, but he never let it slip."

"What did this compound look like?"

He wrinkles his nose. "Nothing impressive. Just a bunch of cinderblock buildings in the middle of nowhere. The only weird thing about them is the way they were lined up. It was hard to see on the ground, but when we would do target practice far away, they connected into a sort-of zigzag."

"Like a Z?"

Out of the corner of my eye, I see Colt lean forward, his eyes bright with interest.

"But with an extra zig."

Colt sweeps his hand through the air. "Like that?"

He nods.

"Why would anyone build a compound like that?" I ask.

"For the planes that would fly over and drop off supplies." Babe stiffens as the color drains out of his face.

"I've told you too much," he says, more to himself than to us.

"What could we possibly do with this information?" I ask like it's a joke. "Ask every man near Albuquerque to show us his forearm? Scout all the planes leaving the airport? See if we can find someone to drive us around the enormous, barren state known as New Mexico and look for W-shaped compounds? Use Google Earth?"

The air grows thick and hot in the classroom as I repeat my words back to myself. I groan, recognizing exactly how Colt and I could find the compound without needing anything beyond a phone and an internet connection.

"Of course we wouldn't do that?" I say in a hurry, but even to my ears, the lie is obvious.

So fast that I'm almost not sure what I'm seeing, Babe jumps up and lurches toward Colt. With more force and finesse than his slight body suggests, he does some fast karate chops at Colt, disarming him. The gun clatters to the floor. In the second it takes Colt to decide if he should go after Babe or the gun, Babe has reached the lectern.

Cursing, Colt grabs his gun and points it at Babe, but he's too late by a quarter of a second. Babe has unzipped the bag and now has a gun—a scary, big one—in his hands. He aims it at us as all the breath whooshes from my body.

Instinctively, I throw my arms in the air as, slowly, Colt does the same, his gun dangling ineffectually from his fingers.

"I need your permission to put my gun down." Colt's voice is soft and steady.

Barely breathing, I brace myself for a hail of fire. My body will be riddled with bullets. I only hope that it will be quick and not too painful.

I chastise myself for getting myself into this predicament. Like

89

the Sixth Street Shooting, I shoulder the blame. But there's one difference this time. I'm here because I wanted to help someone other than myself, make sure that person can stay alive to help the person who needs him.

So I made a baby step forward, which would be something to celebrate, except that I'm going to make the ultimate payment for it.

I glance at Colt, who is looking at me. My heart speeds up, and it has nothing to do with the danger we're in. Although we don't say anything out loud, it feels like we are talking.

"Hey," Babe says.

Together, we peel our eyes away from each other to look at him. My arms drop as my mouth flops open.

He has pushed the barrel of the gun under his chin.

"No!"

I thought it would be a scream, but instead, it comes out of me as a garbled plea.

Babe's hand tightens around the trigger, and he pushes the gun against his temple.

No, no, no. The words pound in my head like a hammer against the same nail.

No one is dying today. Not me. Not Colt. Not Babe. That much I've decided.

Next to me, Colt slowly places his gun on the lectern. He takes off his jacket and pulls out his pockets. "I don't have any more weapons."

"I wish you did," Babe says with a bitter laugh. "Then you could shoot me, and the whole thing would be over."

"I'm not going to shoot you. I only hurt people who hurt other people."

"She stopped me." He jerks the gun in my direction, and I flinch. He swipes it toward Colt, who doesn't budge.

"Maybe I should just kill you both and then turn the gun on myself. It won't be what I was supposed to do, but it will get in the news." He affects a newscaster's voice. "Today, a gunman struck down a young couple at the University of Texas while the rest of the school was watching the Longhorns win their sixth consecutive game."

I blink. "In the news? Why does that matter?"

"That was the only thing that mattered. We were instructed to kill as many people as possible. The charm*ah* told us to pretend it was a video game. The more people we hit, the more points we scored. To be one of the most famous mass shooters, we had to kill lots and lots of people." He laughs wryly. "He left it up to us if we turned the gun on ourselves at the end, but he said he wouldn't recommend it."

"Really?" I ask.

He nods. "Even though we would end up in jail, we'd get three hots and a cot for the rest of our lives. Plus . . ." He shakes his head in wonderment. "Apparently these shooters have groupies. Girls write letters and visit, and guys hold you up as a hero."

"That's messed up," I say.

"It wasn't like any of us had more coming to us."

"But if you shooters stayed alive, couldn't you lead them to the compound?" It's the first thing Colt has said in a while.

Babe shudders at the sound of Colt's voice. Not making eye contact, he says, "The charm*ah* put us all on a bus. Around the country we'd go, one kid getting off at a time to shoot people. I was the second one dropped off."

"Do you know where the other locations are?" I ask. "Or who any of the other boys are?"

"No clue. We weren't allowed to talk to each other, or else we would get pistol-whipped."

His face scrunches up. "Now I have to do something because nothing has gone to plan." He thrusts the gun against his temple. "Everyone will be better off, myself included."

I think fast. This kid has had nothing to look forward to in life. He doesn't want to shoot people but would to save his sister. Even the idea of life in jail doesn't faze him since it wouldn't be worse and maybe even better than his current life.

The people behind this are good in the worst way possible. They understand exactly what strings to pull to make a poor, scared kid dance.

Despite all the things Babe has told us, I don't think he's a bad kid. In fact, a good one is probably in there if he could be given a chance to let it out.

I decide to run with that idea. Remind him of what I was reminded of just yesterday—tomorrow doesn't have to look like today. If he kills himself, then he'll never know what tomorrow could look like.

"Let me," I whisper to Colt. "He's scared of you."

"Ladies first," he says so quietly that I can barely hear him. "But if you rile him up, then I'm ending things."

With Colt's warning in mind, I step out of my heels to make myself shorter than Babe, and I make my face friendly but not too smiley.

"Hey." I squint at his Astros jersey, my brain flaring with a point of entry. "You've been dealt a crappy hand of cards—really crappy. But so were the Red Sox for years and years. How long did they go between World Series wins? Wasn't it like a century or something?"

"1918 to 2004," he says. "The curse of the Bambino. The team sold Babe Ruth to the New York Yankees, and we went from one of the most successful teams in baseball history to being the most disappointed."

I whistle. "Eighty-plus years. That's a long time for a fan to wait for a pennant.

"It is, but when you're a Red Sox fan, you're a fan for life—win or lose."

"Is that because you believe in the team's ability to do better, to keep trying no matter what, to fulfill their promise of today, tomorrow?"

I cross my fingers and wait, hoping he'll put together what I'm saying.

It takes a moment, but his face crumples and he pulls the gun an inch away from his head.

"What happens now?" he asks. "If I put my hands up and give you the gun?"

I look at Colt since I have no idea.

"I've got associates in the area. They'll take you to a decent hotel while we track down this charmer. Once he's out of the picture, you can go back to Boston. My associate will give you a cover story and a couple of hundred bucks to get yourself situated." Colt pauses. "One condition. You can't tell anyone about where you've been or what you were going to do. From here on out, it's like it never happened."

"I can't tell whether you're a good guy or a bad guy," Babe says.

Colt gives him a half-smile. "Somewhere in between."

"What happens to the compound? The kids on the bus?" he asks.

"The compound won't be around for much longer. As for the kids, they'll get back to their homes in a week or so after the charmer is taken care of."

"Will the charm*ah* go to jail?"

"Once we're done with him, he'll wish he were in jail."

"My little sister . . ." Babe presses his lips together. "The charm*ah* is going to be pissed when he finds out this shooting didn't happen. Will he go after her?"

"I'll request a guard for her." Colt smiles. "You're a good brother."

Babe grins as he hands over the gun. "It's a deal."

Colt quickly stows the gun in the duffel bag and slings it over his shoulder. He extends his hand. "Shake on it?"

They pump their hands as I exhale for the first time in a long time.

I make idle chitchat with Babe about the Red Sox's chances this year as Colt goes outside to call people. Once he comes back in, he tells Babe where to go and whom to meet.

I give him a hug. "Be careful out there," I say. "You got a sister who needs you."

When Babe closes the door behind him, Colt turns to me.

"I don't know whether to kiss you or yell at you," he says, the gold in his brown eyes smoldering.

"So I'll decide for you."

I press my lips against his as he laces his arms around me. In a shaft of sunshine that fades from yellow to gray, we kiss, not needing air, just each other.

Until Colt pulls away.

19

C olt's jaw is drawn, but his eyes are soft as he gazes at me.

"That was reckless beyond belief, intercepting a perpetrator. You could have gotten yourself killed," he says.

I shrug. "Maybe. But as soon as I saw him, I knew he didn't want to kill anyone. All he needed was someone to talk him out of it and show him a way forward."

"He was carrying an arsenal in that duffel bag with strict instructions to kill as many people as possible or his little sister would die. Why could you talk him out of it?"

"His shoulders."

I round my shoulders and tuck my head under, like I'm a reluctant turtle, to show Colt how I knew. "This was his posture. That's not the body language of someone who is confident."

Colt tips his head at me. "How do you know so much about body language?"

"My dad. Whip Wainwright didn't get to be one of the successful men in the business by luck. He would study the body language of anybody he was negotiating with and then used it to his advantage. He says movement never lies. He could tell when someone was lying or telling the truth or telling most of the truth while hiding something."

"And he taught you all of this?" Colt runs a hand through his blond hair. "How?"

I close my eyes as his tawny scent hits my nose and then works its way down my body, tickling all the sensitive parts. For a moment, I let it fill me up before remembering I haven't answered his question. I force myself to focus.

"He would take me out to eat. Sometimes to fancy, five-star restaurants and other times to hole-in-the-wall dives. He'd make the meal into a game. We would listen to the conversations around us and contrast them to how the people were moving. The man to my left in a pinstriped shirt might crack jokes to the waitress to show what a great guy he is to his date, but my dad would show me how that same guy wouldn't meet her eyes or interrupted her as she recited the daily specials. In reality, he was a jerk and would stiff her on the tip. At the time, I didn't realize what he was doing, but now I know he was teaching me to get an honest read on people."

My throat gets scratchy. I miss my dad, his booming voice and mane of white hair. That feeling makes me double down on my promise to do something with myself other than fail classes. I want to make him proud of me.

I'm not sure stopping a reluctant mass shooter falls into that category although maybe he'd be proud of my daring. Not that it matters since this will be one of those things that happened but is never talked about. Colt is an assassin, which means his heroics—and mine by extension—remain on the down-low.

"That's a neat trick your dad taught you," he says, the words clipped and hard. "But you should have let me handle the situation. I gave you explicit instructions, Libby."

The gold in his eyes flares, which gives me a pause. He is good looking all the time, but there's something about him when he's riled up that makes me swoon. Maybe it's because he's a man of few words and even fewer movements, but this flash of anger hints at the passion I just know is simmering beneath the surface of him.

He starts to pace back and forth. "In the future, you have to follow my directions. You got lucky this time, but you might not again." He glares at me. "The situation with the kid was a one-off. Another shooter could have turned the gun on you, and it would have been over."

"At least I would have died doing something that was worthy," I burst out. "Anyway, you have Brian. You can't die. He needs you."

He stops mid-stride. "That was your motive?"

I don't answer because I don't know what the right answer is. His tone sounds accusatory, but I'm not sure I understand why.

"Yes, you're needed, and I'm not," I whisper, the words so thin and quiet I'm not sure he hears them floating from me to him. "The situation was clear to me."

Before I have time to think, he's there, sweeping me into his arms. Strong and sinewy, they curl around me, pressing me into him, him into me.

His lips crash down on mine as I, greedy and so hungry, open myself to accept him.

Colt's tongue is soft and probing. It wraps around and strokes mine and laps me up, and I am helpless in my response, which is ardent in its honesty. Around us, the world blurs and then fades away altogether. The only thing that remains is this kiss between Colt and me, which goes on for an epically long time.

If only it could go on forever, but the roar of a crowd outside the window rouses us. The Longhorns have won. That win disturbs our private one, and we open our eyes, bringing our kiss to a close.

As we pull away, slowly, reluctantly, I know one thing.

I have been kissed enough times to know when a kiss means more than just a kiss. This is that kiss.

I stand there, my skin dewing over with the residue of our passion, my heart fluttering like the wings of a hummingbird. My feelings shining in my eyes, I meet Colt's gaze, which is wondering and admiring.

Then, something like a cloud passes in front of his eyes, the gold darkening into the brown, and he's his mysterious self again.

"We need to book tickets to New Mexico," he says.

And just like that, it's as if the kiss never happened.

20

Colt and I are back at my apartment, booking airplane tickets to Albuquerque after pouring over Google Maps for hours to locate the compound. We scrubbed through what felt like every inch of the New Mexico desert before I spied the weird, W-shaped buildings.

Although I'm pretending to be cool about it, I can't stop thinking about our kisses. My knees get weak and watery as I remember the way his lips connected to mine, how that kiss generated more and more electricity until it felt like we could power Austin.

All I want to do is kiss him again and again and again.

Instead, we're pretending like it didn't happen, that we're just business partners with a task to complete.

I peek at Colt, who is lounging at my desk, his long legs stretched out. He should look odd among all the leopard print and girly furniture, but somehow, he seems as if he's right at home.

Although that may be my wishful thinking since he hasn't turned his eyes on me once. He's scrolling through an endless list of flights, checking dates and times of one against all the others.

Finally, he turns away from the computer. "Day after tomorrow. That's when we'll leave for Albuquerque."

"Why the day after tomorrow?" I ask. "Shouldn't we go early tomorrow?"

He shakes his head. "You've got good instincts, but you need to learn to use a gun."

I blink. "A gun. But why? You'll be with me the whole time. Plus, isn't the compound supposed to be abandoned?"

"I won't be with you forever, and you need to prepare for every situation. You're the daughter of a public figure, and a great number of people will threaten you because of that."

Oh. In the wake of the kiss, I'd hoped Colt had forgotten about our deal.

"Even still, what good will a gun do for me?" I point to my purse, which is a small, quilted bag that can hold nothing more than a comb, a credit card, and a tube of lipgloss. "It's not like I've got space to pack heat."

His lips open and close, and for a moment, I think he's about to tell me something important.

He doesn't.

Instead, his mouth sets in a stern line. "You can't predict what will happen. You have to be prepared to defend yourself, whether I'm around or not."

"You could just always be around." I wince at how desperate those words sound.

Fortunately, he ignores me. "It's non-negotiable."

I try to imagine what it would be like shooting a gun. I've never even held one before.

"Is it hard?" I ask. "Learning to shoot a gun?"

"Not if you do what I tell you to do."

Colt turns back to the computer. The conversation is over.

Confident that he's not paying attention, I assume a pose like a gangster, press my fingers together in the shape of a gun, and pretend to shoot. I feel like a Bond girl, sexy and powerful.

"Bang," I say to myself.

"It's not that glamorous," Colt says, without lifting his eyes from the screen.

I scramble out of my stance as my cheeks get burn.

"What is it then?"

"Staying calm and focused. Having a plan and completing it. Most of all, it's about being safe. The goal should be to have no casualties, and if there is one, it should never be an innocent bystander."

"Got it, teach."

With that, I shuffle into my bedroom to pack. I don't know how long it's going to take me to learn to shoot a gun tomorrow, so I might as well get a head start on my suitcase.

"No high heels," he says to my back. "Sensible shoes only. Think sneakers or flat boots. And no dresses or short skirts either. Dress like you might get dirty or have to run for your life."

Feeling like a child, I start throwing clothes on the bed: jeans, T-shirts, and a pair of sneakers. I eye the frumpy pile with distaste.

Maybe Colt will approve, I think as I roll my socks the way Brian showed me earlier. In between the neat cylinders, I slip in a silver-framed picture of me with parents that was taken at my high school graduation. It's one of my favorite pictures because of how happy we look.

"Hey," he calls from the living room. "Libby is short for Elizabeth, right? Do you spell it with an *S* or a *Z*?

I groan—a big, out-loud one. My real name is top-secret, and I give only when I absolutely have to, which these days, means never.

"Why do you need to know?" I ask to buy myself time to think of a way not to tell Colt my real name.

"For the plane tickets. It has to be your legal name."

"Uh . . . my legal name is a little hard to spell. It's easier if I type it myself."

"I'm already at the keyboard."

I start to hum, pretending I don't hear. "Be there in a minute."

"Just spell it." His annoyance hardens the words into pellets that smack at my ridiculousness.

I take a deep breath and let the letters loose as quickly as I can. "C-H-A-B-L-I-S."

"Your legal name is Chablis?" Colt asks. "Like the wine?"

"Sure is." I reach for an enthusiastic tone, trying to pretend that I love being named after the wine my mother drank the night I was conceived.

Colt knocks on the door, even though it's wide open.

"You can come in." I point at the open door. "Obviously."

"I want to be courteous," he says as he lopes in.

Although it's been maybe five minutes since I've seen him, my heart leaps into my throat at the sight of him.

He lounges against the wall, his eyes curious. "How did you get Libby from Chablis?"

"When I was a little girl, I couldn't quite get my tongue around the letters correctly, so it would come out Chalibby. Even once I learned to say it correctly, people smirked when I was introduced. So I switched to Libby, which solved two problems. No one called me Chablis anymore, and everyone thought my real name was Elizabeth."

"Why did you care? It's not like it's the first name that's taken its inspiration from a libation. Brandy comes to mind. I even knew a girl named Cristal."

I roll my eyes. "Classy people don't name their kids after the white wine their mom drank the night she got knocked up by a guy three times her age."

Colt laughs but stops himself after a beat. "I don't mean any disrespect, but it's a funny story." He pauses. "I guess your mom grew up poor."

"She worked as a maid in motels before meeting my dad. She was barely in her twenties when he wined and dined her. The night they . . ." I try to think of an elegant way to put it. "Consummated their relationship and created me, she had tried Chablis for the first time. She thought it sounded so beautiful and unique."

"Does your mom still drink Chablis?"

I shake my head. "Her tastes evolved to more esoteric wines like a sixty-year-old Bordeaux. Unfortunately, she still calls me Chablis even though I've asked her multiple times to stop."

"There's nothing to be embarrassed about," Colt says. "Names don't mean anything. It's the person that matters."

"This coming from a guy who has a dozen-plus names, all of which are fake."

"My real name isn't any better than the fake ones."

For the briefest of seconds, I stare at Colt, the swoop of blond hair dangling over his eye, the ramrod backbone, and I feel like I know him. Not from Austin, but from somewhere long before this. A name dances tantalizingly close to the tip of my tongue, but bows out before I can wrap myself around it.

"You took to Colt pretty quickly," I say to cover my confusion. "Is that because it's your real name?"

He grins, which makes my heart do a couple of cartwheels. "Nope, but I wish it was. Now that's a good name."

"Better than Chablis, that's for sure."

"Can I call you Chablis?" He winks. "But only when you're naughty."

I reach out to playfully push him away, but the touch of my skin to his skin sends an electric pulse through me. His smile fades, him feeling it too. Without thinking, we grab each other, kissing like it's the only way we can communicate.

Until, once again, he pulls away.

"Good night, Libby." He enunciates my chosen name with care.

21

"It's heavier than I expected," I say, moving Colt's gun from hand to hand, the weight of it—real and metaphorical—pressing heavily into my fingers.

Like all the best antiques, this one has only gotten better with age. The metal glows with the patina of a weapon that has been used often and lovingly. I graze my fingertips across the barrel, around the cylinder where the bullets rest, and down the handle.

"The original Colt SAA Peacemaker." He offers a proud smile. "The barrel is 7 1/2 inches, and the gun itself is 13". It's been in my family since the late 19th century. Most people who have them think they're too valuable to shoot, but I say using mine is the best respect I can show it."

"And now, here it is, in my hands. I'm sure it wishes it was locked away in a gun safe somewhere."

Colt doesn't return my jokey smile. "You'll be the first person I've ever let shoot it."

All of a sudden, the gun's weight feels like it increases tenfold in my hand as my heart skips a beat and then another for good measure.

Colt is impossible to get a read on. He kisses me like he means it, but nothing—and I mean nothing—beyond that. After kissing me last night until I thought I might faint, he bid me goodnight to finalize our flight. I was left limp and damp and panting, nothing to do beyond going to bed where my dreams were torrid images of Colt. I woke less rested than when I pulled the covers to my chin.

Now, here we are at a gun range, and I'm still tormented by him: the way his tawny smell embeds itself into me, how he moves with grace and economy.

Realizing that I'm doing it again, living in my fantasy world rather than reality, I force myself to focus on the gun.

"It's beautiful," I say because it's the truth. The gun shimmers in the morning sun, and I appreciate the juxtaposition of the straight barrel to the slope of the handle.

"Terrifying too," I add because, for real, it's a killing machine. Its power feels immense in my hands. One intemperate moment, and I could blow a hole straight through someone.

He nods. "Never forget that. Plenty of people take pride in their guns but have no respect for them. And that's how folks get hurt."

As I stare at the gun, memories from the Sixth Street shooting fill my mind: the screams, the sobs, and the sickening thud of bodies hitting the ground. In quick, jerky steps, I back away.

Colt gives me a sympathetic look. "Sixth Street?"

I stutter an affirmative.

He rubs the gooseflesh on my arms, his warm hands trying to do what will never happen—make me forget. "It's okay."

But I feel like I will never be okay after the shooting.

He places his pointer finger under my chin and rotates my head to meet his eyes. "Breathe. It won't stop you from remembering, but it will remind you that you're okay right now."

Gun still in my hand, I follow his directions to breathe: in and out, in and out. The memory finally moves from the center of my mind to the sidelines. I need to focus on learning to shoot a gun, so we can visit the compound and figure out what sick person is behind this.

"So what do I do?" I strive to keep my voice neutral.

"The first thing—and the one thing you never forget—is to treat every gun as if it's loaded."

"Even if I know it's not?" I peek down the barrel since I know there are no bullets. Colt removed them before handing me the gun.

Colt snatches the gun from me. "It's always loaded, regardless. Which brings me to point two." He points the gun down to the ground. "Always keep your firearm pointed in the direction that will do the least amount of harm."

He hands the gun back to me, which I promptly point to the ground. Colt half-smiles at me. "You're a fast learner. I like that."

I wink. "I have a good teacher."

"Well, that teacher needs to explain a few more things." He takes his hand and places it on top of mine and moves it off the trigger. He bends down until his head is in line with my ear. For a moment, he just breathes as all the air exits me. "Only put your finger on the trigger when you're ready to shoot." He rests his pointer finger over mine and then moves it, centimeter by centimeter, until my finger is over the trigger.

"But since we're not ready to shoot, let's move it off." He glides my finger off of the trigger until it's a safe distance away.

"One last thing," he whispers, tickling the inside of my ear. I shudder as my blood turns into molten gold.

"What's that?" I try to keep my voice steady, but my words come out choked with desire.

"Always be sure of your target, backstop, and beyond." Colt sweeps his gaze around the gun range. "Obviously, this isn't an issue at a place like this. They've already made sure that people and property are out of the line of fire."

I follow his gaze around the gun range. For all the sonic excitement of pops and bams and booms, the place is visually plain. Just stalls bisected by a wood counter where people can lay down their weapons to reload them. A shooter unleashes a rapid stream of bullets. The tattoo makes me shiver as the images of that horrible night flood me again.

"We can stop here if you're feeling traumatized."

I shake my head as I force myself to inhale. "I want to finish something I've started."

That's the truth. I want to do it, to learn to shoot Colt's gun, even hit the bull's eye, prove to myself that I can do something even if it scares me.

"What were you saying about the target, backstop, and beyond?" I ask.

"You've got to scope out more than your target."

"For the other people near them?"

"For the other people near them who you can't see."

Colt catches my confused look. "If you're in the woods, you need to look because trees could obscure people. If you're in a parking lot, you'll need to check if there are folks in cars."

"Got it." I give the gun a small jiggle, trying to go for confidence. "Now how do I shoot this bad boy?"

"You're a beginner, so you'll need a two-handed grip to start." He takes my right hand and wraps it around the handle before pressing my other hand firmly against the exposed portion of the grip not covered by my right hand. "Dominant hand on the back strap. Non-dominant one supporting it. Index finger near, but not on, the trigger."

I memorize the position of my hands in relation to the gun.

Colt points to the way my fingers line up, my right thumb landing on top of my left one. "They should line up like a puzzle."

I nod and then shift from foot to foot, unsure of how I should position my feet. "How do I stand?"

He snuggles in behind me until his body is pasted against mine. With his right leg, he nudges my right leg until it's under my hip. He repeats the process with my left leg. "Bend your knees."

I do, which curls my pelvis forward. His pelvis follows mine as my breath hitches. We fit together like . . . puzzle pieces.

For what must be minutes, we stay like that, curled together.

"Aim," Colt says.

I raise the gun and eyeball the target.

"Press the trigger, but don't yank it."

Slowly, I pull the trigger back.

"Bam," Colt whispers in my ear as he flexes against me. My knees start to buckle, and I stiffen them although, inside, I'm quaking.

"Bullets," I say. "I'm ready for them."

He gives me a quick tutorial on loading the gun and then steps out of my way.

I take an unhurried pace as I follow all the steps he showed me. I close my left eye and let my right eye register the target. Gently, I drag the trigger back.

Bam.

The first shot misses completely as the recoil sends me staggering. I find my form again and take a deep breath.

Bam.

As the bullet pumps from the chamber, I brace my body a little this time, which keeps the gun steady. I grin to myself. The second bullet has hit the target—barely. I don't let that small victory excite me. Instead, I stay focused.

Bam.

The third hits the bull's eye. I ignore it and prepare to do the exact same thing three more times.

Bam. Bam. Bam.

The fourth, fifth, and sixth hit the bull's eye too.

I turn to face Colt, a big smile on my face. "How'd I do, teach?"

22

"You're a natural, I'd say."

Colt has obtained my shooting target and is examining the paper. Four of my six bullets have blown a hole through the center.

As I admire the paper, I internally give myself a self-congratulatory high five. For the first time in a long time, I took on a new skill, saw it through, and executed it—pretty well, too, if the target is any indication.

"You need more practice, but you did better than some people who've been shooting their whole life," Colt flashes me one of those half-smiles that sends my heart skidding across my chest. "We should celebrate."

Suddenly shy, I twiddle with one of my earrings. "Dinner? I'd love to try those short-rib tacos you like so much."

"Done."

He turns to leave, but I tug on his denim jacket. "Can we invite Brian?"

His eyes brighten before resuming their normal inscrutability. "That can be arranged." He nods at my T-shirt, jeans, and sneakers —an outfit picked out and put on by me in hopes of not shooting myself in the face by an unfortunate trip over my high heels. "Why don't we head back to your apartment, so you can get gussied up?"

At the apartment, I toss most of my closet on my bed as Colt waits in the living room. X and O must have stopped by because everything is immaculate, which means I can't find anything.

The one thing I can find is an empty fridge. Normally, it's full to bursting with spicy meals. Those allow me to cry my eyes out while pretending it's the food that's generating the tears, not my emotions. But today, the fridge yawns with nothing but water and a half-opened wine bottle, which is odd. My mom must have told them that I'm at rehab. Shrugging, I'd offered Colt a bottle of water and gotten down to business—looking cute.

I paw through the tangle of clothes on my bed, searching for this backless, one-of-a-kind silvery-blue dress that hits mid-thigh. The dress is too fancy for short-rib tacos, but I don't care about appropriateness right now. This dress has one purpose and one purpose only—to make Colt do more than just kiss me.

I have something I want to tell him, and it will be easier if I do it through my body rather than my words.

"Aha," I exclaim as my fingers close around the elusive garment. I shrug it on and slip into a pair of metallic flats. Dangerous things happen when Colt is around, and I'll be able to run in these.

I planned to put on a full face of makeup, but, as I lock eyes with myself in the mirror, I decide against it. My color is high and my eyes are shining, so I opt for nothing but a swipe of lipgloss.

I open the bedroom door, taking care to step out in slow motion, so hopefully, Colt can appreciate my efforts.

He doesn't say anything, but I don't need him to. His actions say it all. His eyes bug out as his mouth opens and then closes. He offers me the crook of his elbow, which I accept. Although I'm in flats, I walk with poise, my backbone straight, as Colt escorts me to the Barbie-mobile.

Well, the dress was a good idea in concept. In reality, it has proven to be a disaster. After we picked up Brian, we grabbed tacos from the truck and then headed for a street patio to eat them. We picked one attached to a bar that didn't care if we brought food in as long we ordered drinks: wine for me, beer for Colt, and lemonade for Brian.

And that's where the trouble started.

My dress is too short and tight in which to sit comfortably unless I want to flash everyone. The backless style looked cute when I was standing still, but as soon as I try to use my arms, it's a costume malfunction waiting to happen. The slightest breeze balloons the sides out, which means I have to keep my elbows clamped by my side to keep everyone from catching an eyeful of my braless chest.

Like a mechanical doll, I extend my forearm and take my glass of Sancerre. Incrementally, I lift it to my lips and take a small sip before replacing it to the table.

I exhale in relief. I managed to do it without disrupting my dress or spilling a drop. I look up, ready to resume our conversation about how Brian is going to teach me how to make hospital corners with my sheets. Instead, Colt is smirking with me, and my relief turns to embarrassment. He knows exactly what's going on with my dress.

So, pretending I don't notice, I turn to Brian, who has the same affection for short rib tacos as his brother. Both of them have plowed through three and are about to start on taco number four. Mine lay in front of me, untouched. I can't quite figure out how to eat them since they are full to overflowing. Diced tomatoes, pinwheels of peppers, and a slice of avocado rest on top of a mound of beef, all of which are barely contained in tiny corn tortillas. To keep the inevitable spills to a minimum, I have to eat it using two hands.

"Do you not like short rib tacos?" Brian gazes at me, his eyes guileless.

"I'm worried they're too hot for me to handle." I'm worried about no such thing, seeing as I eat X and O's food on a regular basis. But I can't tell the truth because that truth is beyond ridiculous.

"They're a mite spicy, but nothing you can't manage." Colt winks at me. "Come on. Give them a try."

I narrow my eyes at him.

He flashes me an innocent smile.

Brian pipes in. "I like them, and I don't like spicy food. It makes my tummy hurt."

I press my elbows to my side and gingerly reach out to grasp a taco. It's even fuller than I realized, the insides slopping over as soon as my hand squeezes around it.

As I lift it slowly to my lips, wind gusts across the table. My napkin smacks into my face, and my hair flies forward. I can't push them away since my hands are filled with the taco. For a moment, I stay still, hoping the wind will calm down, and my hair and napkin will drift to their original locations.

They don't. And, if this isn't bad enough, something worse happens. A strand of hair starts tickling my nose. The tingling is unbearable, and I cave in. I toss the taco in what I hope is the direction of the table and scratch my nose. The bliss of scratching that itch is interrupted by the sickening thud of my taco in my lap.

Groaning, I yank the napkin off my face to survey the damage. It's bad. The taco landed upside down, and a Rorschach-like blotch is spreading across my lap. Using my napkin, I mop up the mess to the best of my ability.

Finally, I look up, my face scrunched into a tight knot, and brace myself for the laughter I'm sure is coming. But Colt is staring at me, his brow wrinkled. Brian is toggling his head between the two of us.

Colt probably thinks I'm going to throw a massive temper tantrum and disturb Brian. Truth be told, I'd like to. I look like a hot, stupid mess, and I've ruined a beautiful, one-of-a-kind dress that I've worn for maybe an hour. I grab my wine glass, not caring anymore if someone gets a gander of my side boob and take a couple of big swigs. For good measure, I take a couple more, the cool liquid soothing my self-disgust and frustration.

Sulking done, I meet the eyes of Colt and Brian. With a grin, I say, "I said that these tacos were too hot for me to handle, and I was right."

They laugh, and I laugh, and through all the *ha ha*s, Colt catches my eye. He nods at me, the gold in his eyes admiring.

"Cheers to being right," I say.

I lift my glass and clink it against Colt's beer and Brian's lemonade. As we smile at each other, I feel almost foolish with happiness. It's the type that far exceeds the price of a fancy dress.

23

"I'm bummed that I still haven't tried the famous short rib tacos," I say as I kick off my heels. "But it was a fun night all the same."

And it had been fun although my plans to seduce Colt via my sexy dress had failed spectacularly. I wince as I look at my dress with its gigantic stain.

"You were a good sport," he says.

"It was my fault for wearing such a silly dress to eat tacos."

"Maybe, but plenty of girls would be pretty upset and take it out on everyone."

My cheeks get hot as I scrape a circle on the floor with my big toe. "Thanks."

"I mean it, Libby. You surprise me every day."

The words, so honestly offered, catch me surprise, and I tear up. Colt raises his eyebrows questioningly.

"I'm not crying about the dress," I say. "It's just been so long since anybody has said something nice to me that I forgot how good it feels."

"I have lots of nice things to say about you."

"Really?"

He nods. "But words are cheap. Can I show you them?"

"Okay," I say, unsure of what he means.

Colt takes his finger and traces it around the circumference of my face. He goes down my nose and across my lips. He drags it across my cheekbones and circles my ears. His touch is light, almost nonexistent, but I shiver nonetheless. It feels as if he's seeing me through touch.

I come alive in a way I've never before, each nerve he brushes a finger over standing rigid and at attention.

He takes my finger and puts it under his, like he wants to introduce me to myself. Together, we sketch the same path he just did—up and over and around the features of my face.

"Do you feel how beautiful you are?" he asks as we outline my jawbone. "How special you are?"

I can't answer, but at that moment, I feel those things.

He leads our combined fingers down my neck where, briefly, he releases his pressure to unhook my ruined dress. It floats to a silvery blue puddle on the floor. He resumes our position, his finger on top of mine, and dips lower, guiding us both to my most sensitive areas. He loops and swirls and rubs them as the path of curlicues we draw catches fire, leaving me weak and helpless.

Then, he drops to his knees and gently parts my legs. He leaves one hand on top of mine, resting on my heart, which thumps against our clasped hands. It tells us what I already know and what I want him to know.

In a moment of pleasure so exquisite it almost hurts, he finds the center of me. An eddy forms as he spirals his tongue around me and in me. The eddy churns and churns, and I yearn for this to never stop until my body succumbs. The whirlpool disintegrates, spilling through me, sending my blood sloshing. Unable to stand because my body is as weak and helpless as a newborn kitten, I sink to the floor.

Although I'm spent, ready to sleep a dozen hours or so, I want more. To be specific, I want Colt.

As we kneel on the floor, gazing at each other, I can feel him retreat. His chest is drawing back, his weight shifting to his heels.

No, no, no.

I don't know when this opportunity will present itself again, so I reach for him. With my finger, I trace the contours of his lips, so firm and proud, and then trail it down his chest, undoing each button as I go.

Colt stops moving away from me and, instead, tilts his body toward mine. I meet him halfway, and we roll to the floor onto the fuchsia throw rug, him pulling down his jeans and tossing them away.

I throw a leg over him and position myself on top. I want to give to him, to have him give to me, to see the whole thing as it unfolds from a god's-eye view.

I gasp when he enters me. It feels so good, so right, that all I can think of are clichés, like locks and keys and perfectly fitting puzzle pieces, and then I can't think of anything beyond the sensation of our fused bodies moving in harmony. Like a song, it starts off calm and measured before becoming fevered and dramatic. The peak is inevitable, but I hold off for as long as I can.

It's the right choice because the moment takes us together, sending us up and away. I want to watch him, but I'm too caught up in the strata of bliss that keep ricocheting outward.

I fall onto Colt to end with our hearts laying one on top of the other. They throb through our chests, straining toward each other. We don't say anything, but we don't have to do so. Still on the throw rug, he nestles me into his side. With my head on his chest, I fall into a sleep so deep and dreamless that it feels like I'm orbiting in the darkest corner of the universe.

I only wake up because Colt isn't holding on to me anymore. Blinking, I struggle to sit, holding a hand up to shade myself from the sunlight streaming through the windows. Colt stands in front of me, fully dressed, an unreadable expression on his face.

"Time to get going," he says. We have a flight to catch."

24

The flight to Albuquerque is quick, which is good because Colt and I can't seem to look straight at each other. Our interactions are polite but stilted, like we're two coworkers traveling together for the first time.

In a way, that's true since, technically, I'm paying Colt for his time. On my fingers, I count the days we've spent together. I have several fingers left over. Maybe, if everything continues the way it has, I might be able to convince him that I'm not just looking for some quick fun, that we have long-term potential.

Of course, that would require us to act like last night happened. Instead, Colt is dragging both of our suitcases to the small gray rental sedan as he avoids my gaze.

"There's a pileup on I40," he says in a stiff voice. "It's going to be a long trip."

I shrug. "We get there when we get there. It's not like anybody is waiting for us."

Taking scrupulous care to keep a wide berth between us, Colt opens the car door for me and adjusts the seat, so I can stretch out my legs.

"In case you want to take a nap," he explains.

I'm way too amped up to take a nap as I discover after tossing and turning in the cramped seat. All I can think about is last night, particularly with Colt beside me, his tawny smell wafting around the tight contours of the car.

I sit up and gaze out the window for a while, but New Mexico —while stunning in its spare, scraggly beauty—doesn't offer much contrast. So I look up and count the puffy white clouds that appear like stretched-out cotton balls, but I get bored of that too. Finally, I reach for my phone.

The screensaver is a picture of me with my parents on a beach vacation we'd taken a few years earlier. My throat gets hot and scratchy. It's been years since we've done something fun as a family. Feeling more homesick than I have in a long time, I decide to visit some of the newspapers and magazines under the Whip Media umbrella. Although I've never been a big newsreader, my dad's company has won multiple awards for its journalism.

For over an hour, I scroll through article after article, unaware of anything, including Colt. The Sixth Street shooting has top billing along with articles examining Alexander Benoit's brief life. A new supreme justice has been nominated, so that means many articles are devoted to gun control and the death penalty. The articles, regardless of their slant, are written in a dramatic, over-the-top tone.

Daddy always said it's important to play both sides since that's twice as many customers. But I never thought this is what he meant. Every article I read seems designed, regardless of its slant, to sow dissension—if the comment sections are anything to go on.

If you agree with the article's content, then you're screaming about how right the author is. If you disagree, then you're screaming at those who agree. Regardless of your side, everyone uses the same weapons: name-calling, bullying, and childish memes. Toddlers in the midst of a meltdown are more civil than these commenters.

"What do you think about gun control?" I ask Colt abruptly.

He glances at my lap where my browser is open to a bombastic article about how gun control is the only thing that will stop mass shootings. The author is persuasive, but how can I be persuaded when the article I read before this at a different publication argued the opposite, just as persuasively. The only thing the two articles have in common is the supreme conviction of their opinions.

"Wouldn't hurt, probably wouldn't help," he says.

"I'm not sure I follow."

"Guns are a symptom of the problem rather than the problem." He shrugs. "That being said, making guns more difficult to access might stop some hot-heads. As for the rest who plan it out months in advance, they'll turn to gasoline and matches or build their own bombs."

"What's the problem?"

He juts his chin at my phone, which is going dark. "What do you think the problem is?"

I don't know the answer to *that* beyond America seems to have a lot of people in rage and pain, so I change the subject. "My dad always said politics is a sporting event for the common man."

"That's a clever way of putting it."

"What he meant is that, once you get to a certain threshold in personal wealth, politics don't matter. If the government raises taxes, then he'd move his money to another country. None of the laws would ever apply to my dad because he could always buy his way out." I look out the window again at the scraggly bushes, which are interrupted every hundred feet or so by colorful billboards.

"Did your dad say anything else?" Colt says it easily enough, but his eyes are alert. He seems interested, more than he should be in a casual conversation about my dad's political beliefs. I shrug, chalking it up to him trying to erase the weirdness that's sprung up between us after our night of . . . I flush as I remember how astonishing it had felt when we'd come together.

"He says . . ." I twist my earring, trying to gather my thoughts. "Well, he believes the rich people who give money to politics know the laws they get passed don't affect them. They just want to play god and force everyone to live their opinions. It's all wrapped up in their egos."

"He's not wrong about that."

"What do you think?" I ask.

Colt doesn't say anything for a long time. Maybe his job has given him an even dimmer view of politics and people than my dad's. I'd almost given up on him answering when he responds.

"We've become overly sensitized to competition and desensitized to compromise." He keeps his eyes on the road even though there's not a single automobile near us. "You can blame it on everything from the obsession with winner-take-all reality shows to the constant spin cycle of the news. Plus, these forums act as echo chambers for people to air their viewpoints and be applauded for whatever noxious ones they hold. So many folks have gotten it into their heads that if they give an inch, then they've lost everything. Compromise means your opinion has to accommodate other opinions, which means giving a couple of inches here, so you can get a mile there. That's part of the reason my job isn't going anywhere anytime soon."

Colt exhales and offers me a half-smile. "That was a lot of words for a strong and silent type like myself."

I return his smile as I think through his answer. "Are you planning on being an assassin for the rest of your life?"

"I haven't decided." He laughs without humor. "I fell into it by accident, but I've stayed by choice."

"How did the Pact find you? Or did you find the Pact?"

"I spent a lot of time at the gun range, honing my skills, working through my teenage angst. Someone—to this day, I don't know who—noticed my talent and recommended me."

"It was that simple?"

"It was."

His tone has the ring of finality, so I change the subject.

Kind of.

"Is there career advancement for assassins?"

He nods. "I could move up to management position and be in charge of a couple of guys like myself."

I laugh. I have to. Even assassins can't escape corporate hierarchies.

"How do you move up?"

"I'd have to do something big and impressive that's outside my normal job duties. Something that shows my creativity and intelligence."

"Like what?" I ask.

"Like find out who's behind this compound."

"And once you do that, does this promotion come with a corner office? A better parking space?" I giggle, so he knows I'm teasing.

"A pay bump is the carrot. It would mean I'll be able to afford Brian's care with no worries. Also, it'd be less risky but more stress. I would be the guy who tells a guy to take another guy's life." He pauses. "Have you heard of the trolley problem?"

I think back to an ethics class I'd taken at the college in Vermont. I'd sat in the back row as the professor and the other students engaged in fevered discussions about right and wrong. Some of it had sunk in, mostly because everyone had been so loud.

"Is that the one where there are five people tied up on one track? I could pull a switch and divert the trolley onto another track where I'd kill one person related to me."

During the debate, people were yelling at and over each other. Some were convinced that it was a moral obligation to save as many lives as possible while others argued that, simply by participating, it became morally wrong since no one would be at fault if you left the trolley on its original track.

"That's the one."

"My professor said it's a thought experiment to get you in touch with your values."

"I live it every time I'm called up," he says. "I believe it's better to take one life than let that one life take many lives."

"How do you deal with taking a life?"

"Technically, I'm following orders, but the Pact allows me to back out if I have a good reason."

He veers off the highway to an almost unnoticeable side road. For a while, he says nothing as I turn his words over in my mind. What would I do in that situation if I had to kill one person to save more than one person?

I have no idea.

Then, as we approach the compound, he says, "I've never backed out. Not even thought about it."

25

The compound reeks of evil. The cinderblock buildings are dingy and covered in stains that, if the big fenced pen off to the side indicates, must be from dog pee. *No Trespassing* signs litter the scrubby yard, and I flinch looking at the windows. Some are riddled with bullet holes.

The only positive thing I can say is that it looks deserted.

"Nothing good happened here," I say.

"You're right about that." Colt loops the car around the weirdly arrayed buildings. From above, they may resemble a W, but up close, they just look shoddily constructed, like it was too much effort to put them in a straight line. It seems like someone threw them up as quickly and cheaply as possible.

"Better safe than sorry," he says as we drive in slow motion around the compound. "If some creep is loitering, we can make a fast getaway."

He parks the car under the shadow of the largest building. "Get in the driver's seat. I'm going to do a quick look-see." He holds a hand up as I open my mouth to argue with him. "If everything is clear, then you can come inside. I doubt, though, there's anything you're going to want to see, but it's your choice."

I wait for what feels like an eternity for Colt to return although, in reality, it's not more than a few minutes.

He throws open the car door for me. "All clear." He grabs a couple of bags from the backseat. "In case we find something worth keeping that could identify who's behind this."

We push open the front door and step inside. Colt flips a switch, which brightens the room from pitch black to dark gray. Although I can't see much, I can smell plenty, and it's all unpleasant. I gag when the stench of feces overtakes me.

He lopes ahead and hits another switch, casting the room into a fluorescent whiteness. Once I see what's there, I wish Colt had left the space in darkness. A few broken chairs lay overturned on the grimy floor, and a checkered table cloth hangs forlornly over a long, spindly table. It must be the canteen where the boys ate their meals, but I can't imagine how anyone ate anything in this space because dried blood is splattered everywhere. Beatings must have accompanied their meals.

Although my stomach is mostly empty, nausea overtakes me. What a horrible place. I think of Babe. I hope he's somewhere safe with a hearty meal to tuck into.

"Let's move on," Colt says.

So we do, through a dorm of busted metallic bunk beds and a locker room of overflowing toilets and clogged-up showers.

"Poor boys," I say. "This place is worse than a hellhole."

He nods grimly as we enter another building. This one, although not clean by any stretch of the imagination, at least possesses functioning furniture. A splintery desk sits in the center with papers piled high and open binders.

"Bingo," Colt says under his breath.

I raise my eyebrows at him.

"Nothing," he says, but the gold in his eyes glints with purpose.

He passes me a bag. "Grab everything. We'll look at it later."

I toss papers and binders into my bag, trying hard to restrain my curiosity. My heart is thumping so loudly in my ears that I don't hear the sound of a car crunching over gravel at first.

Colt holds a finger to his lips as I begin to shake. The car's engine stops. Whoever is here must have seen our car.

In a voice so low I can hardly hear him, he says, "Follow me. Stay down and keep quiet." He hands me his bag and pulls out his gun.

Trying not to whimper, I follow him out of the office, my body hugging the grubby cinderblock wall. My T-shirt becomes streaked with dirt and pee, but I'm way more concerned about staying alive. Colt jerks his head to a small lean-to in between the buildings. We slip inside just in time.

A slender guy wearing a sweat-stained T-shirt comes into view. A faded tattoo of a hissing snake winds up his forearm. And, just like Babe said, one of his feet points in. The slant is so pronounced it looks as if he had a broken bone that was set improperly.

It's the charm*ah*.

Colt curses under his breath as my hands holding the bags go clammy.

"I know you're here," the charm*ah* shouts as he shakes a gigantic, military-grade gun in our direction. "It's just a matter of time till I find you and blow you to bits." He hurls open the office door and steps inside. His crooked foot hits the floor loudly, creating a fe-fi-fo-fum rhythm.

My legs tense.

"Run," Colt says.

We are halfway to the car when the office door swings open. I double my speed as Colt aims his gun over his shoulder.

"I see you!" the charm*ah* screams.

Colt fires, but the charm*ah* anticipated a gun being pointed in his direction. He's already ducked into the lean-to, which gives us just enough time to reach the car. I fling open the car door and throw the bags into the backseat, but it's too little, too late. The charm*ah* is lifting his weapon in our direction.

Colt jams the key into the ignition as the charm*ah*'s finger closes around the trigger. There's not enough time for us to get out of here before the charm*ah* unleashes a hail of bullets on us. Even if he doesn't get us first, he'll get the car and then us.

Then I remember the charm*ah*'s crooked foot and how Babe said he'd trip over it when surprised. So I do the only thing that comes to mind. I yank my shirt up, unclip on my bra, and shake my breasts at him.

Whatever the charm*ah* was expecting, it wasn't that. His jaw drops, and his eyes pop out of his head. As if in a trance, the gun drops to his side, and he walks a few steps toward me before tripping over his turned-in foot. His gun goes flying, releasing a few bullets that skitter harmlessly across the ground, as he face plants.

I jump into the car as Colt zooms out of the compound. The charm*ah* scrambles to his feet and grabs his gun, but it's too late. By the time he's gotten it aimed at us, we're zipping onto the highway, laughing at how silly the charm*ah* looked when he fell over his feet.

"Takes one klutz to know another's literal downfall," I say. I giggle although the emotion I feel the most is relief.

The drive to the airport and the flight back to Austin are endless. Neither of us says much although there's plenty to say. We're too fixated on what's in the bags.

We finally arrive at my apartment.

We should be exhausted, seeing as we flew roundtrip to Albuquerque and escaped from a sweaty madman whose undoing was a pair of boobs.

Instead, I'm humming with energy as is Colt. Neither of us mentions dinner or taking a shower.

"Here goes nothing." He dumps the contents of one bag out on the fuchsia throw rug. I flush as I remember what we did last night on that throw rug. Maybe once we identify what awful person is behind the compound, we can celebrate in the same way.

We paw through the papers, our excitement turning to disappointment the more we investigate. There's nothing notable to see, just a jumble of receipts from a grocery store and an online firearms company.

The next bag yields better results. We find dossiers of the boys with their names, ages, locations, and immediate family. We also find a spreadsheet of planned mass shootings.

I jab at the spreadsheet as the columns organize themselves into understanding. "Look. There's a mass shooting scheduled for tomorrow in Tucson at a big golf tournament." My breath starts coming in tight, short bursts. "Can you stop it?"

He reaches for his phone. "Calling it in now." He tips his head in the direction of the last bag. It appears the least promising, just a dingy binder with a couple of papers inside. "Why don't you open that one?" he says over his shoulder.

I cross my fingers. Maybe this grungy binder will yield the information to get Colt that promotion he wants. A big smile cracks my face. And since I have been instrumental in that promotion—I don't show my breasts to everybody, particularly gross criminals—then maybe this will move our relationship from ending in a few days' time to never-ending.

With those happy thoughts bouncing through my head, I reach for the binder and open it, not expecting to be confronted with a name I know as well as my own. My mouth drops open, and my head flies back from the shock. The invoice is for the compound's operating expenses, billed to Whip Media from the New Mexico School for Wayward Boys. The logo is unmistakable, a large W made to look like a whip.

I know what it means. I just can't accept it. I flip through all the invoices, about two dozen in total, hoping that each one will prove me wrong.

They don't. And, even if I wanted to doubt, the last and most current invoice has a check paper-clipped to it, which has been signed by no one other than my father, Whip Wainwright.

Blackness shrouds my eyes, and I struggle to maintain consciousness. Fortunately, Colt walks in at that moment.

"Libby," he exclaims. "Head between your knees."

I dip my head below my knees as he runs to the kitchen and then reappears with a glass of water.

He maneuvers me onto the high heel shoe chair and pushes the glass between my lips. "Drink."

I slurp the water although I'm shaking too much to get much down. After a few more sips, the blackness clears.

"What's wrong?" he asks, his forehead puckered with concern.

I gesture to the binder. "My dad. Whip Media is behind the shootings." I can barely get the words out, the shock making my tongue heavy and slow.

I look up at Colt, expecting to see natural responses: sympathy for me, surprise at the culprit. Instead, his eyes are gleaming, and he's grinning to himself. Then he feels my eyes on him and quickly organizes his face into one of incredulity.

But it's too late.

"You knew!" I scream. "You knew the whole time."

26

I start crying with such force I'm surprised I can think as clearly as I can because the hurricane streaking down my face is an epic mess of snot, tears, and honks.

"You've been using me." My outraged tone drops to a whisper. "I thought you liked me."

"It can be both things. I was using you, and I liked you."

I can't wrap my head around that because I can't figure out how he'd done it. I was the one who'd chased after Colt, paid him to spend time with me, and did the reckless things to impress him.

"How . . ." I can't finish the sentence because I'm not sure what to ask. Manipulate me into thinking that I was manipulating him? That sounds about right, but I made all those decisions myself. Didn't I?

"I knew who you were long before you knew who I was," he says.

"You did?"

"The Pact sends out territory-specific emails every week with information we might find useful."

"What kind of information?"

"Wealthy or well-known people passing through who might be targets. Local politics that may rile up tempers. The approach of a

135

big sporting event or concert. One day, your name popped up with a short paragraph about how Whip Wainwright's daughter was repeating her junior year at UT."

"Did you already suspect . . ." I can hardly get the words out of my mouth; that's how much I can't believe it. "Whip Media was behind it?"

"I suspected that a media company had to do with the uptick in mass shootings. Whip Media seemed the likeliest candidate. I figured I had nothing to lose by getting to know you so that I could ask a few questions."

I should ask Colt why he thought Whip Media seemed the most likely candidate—a hunch born out by the proof in that binder—but instead, all I can think about is myself.

"Getting to know me?" I ask. "But I chased after you."

"That was by design."

I angrily wipe tears from my eyes. "By design?"

He nods. "I timed all those walks in front of you at the coffee shop. I made sure you saw me and that you knew my routine." He chuckles to himself. "You sure did see me."

"What about the ID I found?"

"I dropped that on purpose. I figured it would give you the motivation you needed to go from looking at me to talking to me. But, by the time you caught up to me, I'd gotten word that a mass shooter was on his way. That's why I was rude to you."

"You pointed a gun at me in my own apartment."

"Sorry about that. But the coincidence seemed too perfect for me to ignore. I thought for sure you knew."

"But how did you know that I would offer to pay you for a week?"

"That was my good luck. When I planned to leave the first time, I knew you knew nothing. If I needed to follow up, I would . . ." He stops to make quotation marks with his fingers. "'Bump' into you at the coffee shop. But then you made your offer. I figured I had nothing to lose." He reaches for my hand, which I pull away. "But I had everything to gain, and that's the truth. I should be paying you for all your help."

I ignore Colt, so I can replay our time together in my head. At the end of the mini-movie, I want to kick myself. It had been right there if I'd bothered to look for facts beyond my feelings. The way he'd run hot and cold, how hard he listened anytime I talked about my dad. Worst of all, the compliments and kisses I'd thought were given as a show of his affection had just been a tactic to keep me off my toes and my head in the clouds.

My emotions blaze into shades of red: the scarlet of shame, the cherry red of anger, the burgundy of self-disgust for not realizing the man I liked was playing me the whole time. They sweep through me until I'm literally seeing red.

"I spilled my guts to you and kissed you and put my life on the line for you," I screech like a dragon breathing fire.

"I didn't expect it to go like this." He gazes at me, the gold in his eyes pleading. "I didn't expect to like you so much."

I want to hit things—Colt, myself, the stupid high heel shoe chair I'm sitting on that perfectly symbolizes my ridiculousness. I go for the chair, pummeling it with all my might. That feels so good that I hit it until I wear a hole in it. As the stuffing pokes through, my anger fades away. I lean back on the chair, tired and so, so sad.

"Were you ever going to tell me?" I hate how broken and desperate I sound, so I force myself to sit up straight and rephrase the question as a statement. "You weren't ever going to tell me."

He clears his throat. "No good would come from you knowing."

My mouth is sour and my stomach is roiling, but I ignore their warnings. "You were going to keep using me until you could get close to my dad. Then, when it was all said and done, you were going to walk away, having gotten what you wanted, no concern for me."

"Right." He pauses. "And wrong."

"No more lies, please."

He shakes his head. "I wasn't going to leave."

I laugh. Does he think I believe that? Who'd want to stay with a girl so dumb she didn't realize she was a puppet?

"It can be both things," he says again. "I could be using you and falling for you at the same time, which adds up to one confusing scenario."

"You have the equation wrong. Because one negates the other. No matter how much you liked me, you used me first."

I gaze around my apartment with its idiotic decor. I had actually thought I was getting myself together here. Instead, I'd made one of the worst mistakes of my life. My eyes land on that mistake, and my body tenses.

I look down at my shoes. I'm still in my sneakers, which means I can run.

So I jog to my desk, pull out my checkbook, and scribble a check. I grab the binder with the Whip Media invoices, and I sprint out of the apartment, throwing the check over my shoulder at Colt.

Then I run—as fast and as far as I can.

I don't trip once. Not even when Colt calls for me to come back.

27

I stand before the front door of my parents' house. After the horrible revelations from Colt, I'd run to the Barbie-mobile and driven to Connecticut, the hours and hours it took for me to get from there to here bleeding into one searing image of me speeding down the road as I cried and cried. Even my phone buzzing with calls from X and O went ignored.

Colt didn't call. Because he'd already gotten everything he wanted from me.

After punching in the security code (my birthday plus my parents' wedding anniversary), I reach for the doorknob and turn. The door, though, is enormous and heavy to boot, so nothing happens. I lean in with all my weight until it swings open with an unexpected force. I tumble into the entryway, which is pitch black and deathly quiet.

"Way to make an entrance, Libby," I mutter as I straighten up.

I look around, trying to remember where the light switch is. It's odd the lights being off and the house silent. Usually, they're blazing, and I'd hear one of the many staff members moving about.

I feel my hand along one wall and then the next before I remember that the switch is hidden behind an ornate vase. Relieved, I flip it on, and the hall floods with light.

I look around, taking in the sights I haven't seen in several years. The last time I was here was for my birthday, spoiling for a fight. I hated the New York women's college I was attending, and I wanted to work at Whip Media. After a knock-down, drag-it-out fight, the compromise was that I could transfer to another college —which didn't work out at all.

I pick up a picture of my high school graduation. I'm standing in between my mom and dad, my arms thrown around them. We look happy and so confident, like the world is our oyster that's seeded with endless pearls.

"Times change," I say as I thrust the picture back down. Dust flies into my nose, and I sneeze.

That's odd. More than odd, in fact. The home may be huge, but it is never, ever dirty. Multiple maids scrub each room, whether it's being used or not, every single day. My mom had hardscrabble beginnings, and to her, dirt equals poverty. She has sworn she will die or break the law before being dirty and poor again.

I look around again, zooming in on the expensive artworks and jewel-encrusted tchotchkes. Dust coats everything, and shiny objects are now dull and tarnished.

Something is wrong—very, very wrong. I flashback to the binder from the compound. Does this filth have something to do with the fact that Whip Media has been funding a compound that trains serial killers?

This makes me remember Colt, which is a terrible thing to remember. My chest constricts, and I put my hands on it to keep my heart in place. I force myself to erase him from my mind. I don't want to think of him again, much less feel for him.

I walk to the end of the entryway and look in both directions.

Who should I see first? I could go left to my mom's sitting room or right to my dad's office.

Neither is going to be pleased to see me since their impression that I'm in rehab while completing the spring semester via distance learning will be exposed for what it is—a baldfaced lie.

I wish I had something positive to tell them, but I don't. I plan to tell a version of the truth. I fell for an assassin who murders for good, and while hanging out with him, I discovered that Whip Media had been cutting checks to a compound that trained shooters.

Then, I would wait for my dad to tell me what I already know, which is that this is the first he's heard of the checks. He'll get right on to sussing out who would do such a thing. My dad has more integrity than anyone I know. He wouldn't—no, he couldn't—fund a domestic terrorist organization.

What kind of person would even do that, fund the training of teenagers to kill other people all in the name of profit?

Not my dad. That I know for a fact. I'd put my money on John Spencer IV. He's been stuck as second in command for over a decade. He has the money to buy my dad out, but my dad would never sell his shares.

Determined, I turn right.

My dad's study is usually a hive of activity. Although he goes into the office several times a week, technology has allowed him to spend more time at home with my mom. Even still, assistants are always buzzing around, phones are jingling, and emails are pinging.

Now, as I push the door open, silence greets me. The study—all dark wood and oxblood leather furniture—is dim save one green-globed lamp glowing. An army cot is set up in a corner.

"Daddy," I say uncertainly.

It takes a minute for my eyes to adjust to the shadows before I see him and gasp. He's slumped in a wheelchair, his previously thick head of white hair now thin and scraggly.

He perks up as I approach.

"Come into the light, little lady," he says in an oily tone that sounds nothing like his normal avuncular one.

I sidle in front of him as my heart cracks wide open. Wrinkles crosshatch his face, and a stringy body I don't recognize has folded in on itself.

I'd always known my dad was older than the average dad. He'd had me at fifty-seven when my mom was all of twenty-two.

But he'd never acted old. He'd always been busy and full of life. Besides the fact he had white hair, which was thicker than plenty of men half his age, I'd never thought about it.

Immediately and even more deeply, I regret not spending more time with him. In the last five years, I'd seen him about that many times, and it has been zero times in the last two years.

I'd thought he would live forever when the reality is that he might not live out the year.

"Daddy," I say again, my voice high and shaky. "I came home because I miss you so much."

My dad rolls his chair closer.

"Well, well, well." He leers as I take a step back.

"A pretty girl I haven't met," he says, baring his teeth.

"Daddy, it's . . . Chablis." I give in and use my real name so undone by this stranger in front of me.

"Chablis. Now that is a lovely name. You're a Chardonnay without all the oak." He ogles me again, his eyes lingering on my breasts. "But that's not a problem because I can bring the hardwood to the occasion."

I step back. "Daddy, it's me, your daughter."

His eyes find mine, and they see me as if they've never seen me before.

"I don't have a daughter," he says. "I'm Whip Wainwright, and the day I get married is the day I die."

Feeling like I've stepped into some warped time-space continuum, I turn on my heel. I run out of the room and straight down the hall to my mom's sitting room.

Except, when I push open the door, it's not a sitting room anymore.

2 8

"Mommy," I say as I stumble into what used to be my mom's sitting room where she would read magazines and shop online.

Things have changed. It looks the way my dad's office used to. Computer screens are crammed on a big, manly, mahogany desk, and multiple phones are lighting up and buzzing. It's an odd sight among all the delicate, cream-colored furniture.

My mom is standing by her porcelain dolls. She holds one with blond ringlets in her arms and is rocking it. I know that doll. It's the one that was specially made to look like me as a baby.

"Shh," she whispers as a phone sounds shrilly. "You got to stop your cryin' now, dumplin'. It worries Daddy."

I should be shocked, having never seen my mother rocking a doll, but I can't process that now. All I can think about is my crazy encounter with my dad.

"Daddy doesn't know who I am," I shriek. "And he tried to hit on me."

My mom looks up from the doll she is holding. She blinks a few times as if she's trying to figure out where she is and who I am.

"Mommy!" I plead.

She places the doll back on the shelf and then turns her

attention to the phone. She lifts the receiver for a brief second. After hearing the voice on the other end, she says, "Not now, John." She slams it down. Without acknowledging me, she picks up a cloth and begins to wipe down the monitor. The cleaning seems to invigorate her, and she lifts her eyes to me.

"Chablis," she says flatly before swiping the cloth over the printer.

My eyebrows raise. My mother does not clean. For as much as she despises dirt, I've never seen her wipe up even a minor spill. She always calls for one of the maids.

"What's wrong with Daddy?" I ask. "Is he okay?"

My mom folds the cloth into a neat square before placing it off to the side. She puts on her reading glasses and pulls out a few papers. Frowning, she makes notes on a few documents. She adds a little curlicue to the beginning of the W of Wainwright, like a schoolgirl.

"Mommy," I whisper. "What's going on? Why is Daddy in a wheelchair? Why is all of Daddy's stuff in here?"

She places the pen down. "Daddy had a stroke almost to the day that you flounced in here and told us that the women's college you were attendin'," she goes for the dramatic screech of a teenager, "had crushed your spirit and you were rich anyway, so why did you have to go to college when you could party with your friends in Monaco."

Tears quicken to the surface. "Daddy had a stroke? Why didn't you tell me?"

My mom glares at me. "Why didn't you ever call for a reason other than to let us know that you were failin' out of school or needed money?"

"I . . ." I trail off. I don't have a good reason beyond I was disappointing them anyway, and I didn't want to needle an already bruised relationship.

"You never think about anyone but yourself."

"I'm trying to change?" I say it more as a question. "The shooting . . ."

She rolls her eyes. "I've heard that one before. Let me guess, rehab didn't work out."

I shake my head. This is not the moment to tell my mom that I made up going to rehab, so I could pay a guy to hang out with me for a week. A lying, backstabbing guy who blew my heart into a million and one pieces.

And once again, I'm thinking of Colt. I force myself to focus on my mom, who's turned her attention back to the paperwork spread in a half-moon in front of her.

"Is Daddy going to be okay?" I twist my hands. "Tell me, please."

"He's in a wheelchair and doesn't know who you are. What do you think, Chablis? Is he goin' to be okay?"

I grip a cloud-colored chair with my hand. "Can you tell me what happened?"

She gazes at me for a moment before placing her pen in a neat line on the paperwork. "Ten minutes, and then I got to get back to work."

"Back to work?" I repeat.

She nods. "The board knows Daddy has been in decline, but not the size of it. To keep our shares safe, I've been standin' in for him. They think Daddy tells me what to do."

"What decline? Does that have something to do with the stroke?"

"Daddy has had memory problems for years. The stroke just aggravated it."

"But Daddy always was on top of everything."

This is true. I never noticed my dad forgetting things, but that might be because I was never around to notice.

"There's a reason for that." She tries to narrow her eyebrows, but the effect is minimal due to all the Botox she's had injected over the years.

"What reason is that?"

"You, Chablis, are the apple of Daddy's eye, and he would be horrified if he knew you'd seen him like this. For the longest time, he would somehow pull himself together for you, and by the time

145

he was too far gone to do that, you weren't around much, and when you were, you couldn't see past your self."

I wipe my eyes, which are wet with tears and regret.

"This is hard for you to hear, but Daddy will not be around for much longer. I suggest you give him your love and then go dally about. You're pretty good at that."

"I'm not going to dally about," I say although I'm not sure what I am going to do.

She laughs meanly. "Don't play me. I know you're failin' again."

"How do you know that? Grades haven't been posted yet."

"Ximena and Orpita told me that your textbooks only gather dust."

"They did?" My eyes go wide as I put it together. My mother had hired X and O to spy on me. Of course, I'd made it easy for them by never bothering to leave when they came over, just assuming they were at my apartment to do what they'd been hired to do—cook and clean.

I press my hand against my heart. That must've been why they showed up right after I called to tell my mom about the shooting. She'd sent them to verify my story and get a read on Colt.

I swallow hard. I am a pawn in everyone else's game, including my own.

"I was comin' from a place of motherly love," my mom says. "You could do anything you put your mind to if you would just put your mind to it."

I trace a circle with my toe. "I'm going to do better. I know I've said that before, but this time, I mean it."

"You'll do what you want, not that it matters anymore."

"Of course, it matters. I don't want to be a rich loser forever."

"Well, I got news for you," my mom says. "You're not rich anymore. Neither are we. We're as poor as church mice. All the staff has been let go, and I'm goin' to sell the house as soon as your father passes." She thumps her palm on the desk. "Knock wood that I can keep the roof over our heads until then. I can't let Whip

Wainwright die the same way he came into the world—in a filthy shack without a cent to his name."

I drop into a chair, my legs suddenly too wobbly to hold my weight. "What?"

"Whip Media has been bleedin' money for years. Your father had plenty of success in his youth, but the world changed and he couldn't keep up once the internet ate print subscriptions and movie tickets. As his mind softened, his brilliance became stubborn ignorance." She sighs. "And like all men in that situation, he grew more and more stubborn that nothing was wrong with him or the company."

"I didn't know," I whisper. "If I had, I would have cut back on my spending."

"In one of his last lucid moments, your father made me promise I wouldn't tell you." She sweeps a hand around the room. "Even as I live like this, with no staff, doin' my own cleanin', he wouldn't hear of you changin' your lifestyle. He wanted his little girl to have the moon and all the stars around it."

The mention of stars makes me remember the mom of my childhood, before the plastic surgery and the hair extensions and the heavy-handed makeup. She would sing "Twinkle, Twinkle Little Star" to me over and over when I was three and terrified of the dark.

"No matter how dark it is, there's always a star twinklin' for you somewhere," she'd say as she pulled the covers up to my chin and around my ears, just the way I like them.

Remembering this unzips all the emotions I've been trying to contain, and I double over in huge, hulking cries.

My mom passes me a tissue, which I soak through. She keeps passing me tissues until I can't cry anymore.

"It's a lot to take in," I say as an explanation.

She nods. "I've had years to adjust, but you've got to reckon with the new reality."

"Which is what?"

"You're goin' to have to make your own way in the world.

That's why your father and I pushed college, neither of us havin' had that advantage in our lives." She gives me a pointed look. "At least, it would prove that you aren't just another rich, worthless girl. We don't got many favors we can call in these days, but a college degree would show that some of your father's smarts had rubbed off on you. Someone could've been wheedled into givin' you a chance."

I flinch at my mom's words. They ring just a little too close to the truth for me to dismiss them. Although I've done some pretty impressive things over the last week, they aren't exactly the kinds of things that look good on a résumé.

Plus, there's that other part about how I was gullible enough not to realize I was being manipulated the whole time. I push thoughts of Colt away.

"Why didn't you tell me I needed to go to college, so I could get a decent job?"

"We did tell you, many times if I remember right, but you've never been able to see past that, at twenty-five, you get a trust fund."

"Do I still have a trust fund?" I squeeze my eyes shut and triple cross my fingers. I've lived my entire life centered on the notion that, at twenty-five, I would have enough money to do whatever I wanted. I have no idea how to navigate a world where that may not be true anymore.

29

My mom doesn't answer me. Instead, she picks up a can of furniture polish, sprays some on a cloth, and polishes the desk, which looks like a literal bull in a china shop, its huge contours dwarfing all the elegant porcelain dolls.

"I'm tryin' to keep up with the dirt, but I keep failin'," she offers as an explanation.

I twist one of my studs with more force than I intended, thanks to my nerves. It pops off into my hand, and I quickly screw it back in, my fingers shaking. I may need to hock these earrings to pay for food.

"Did you hear me?"

My mom places the furniture polish down and settles herself behind the desk. "You still got a trust fund, but I wouldn't expect much from it. Daddy hasn't made a deposit in years, and the market has been down for about as long. I imagine there's enough in there to set yourself up for a simple life, but don't count on first-class plane seats or luxury cars."

I rub my arms, which are pimpled with gooseflesh. My worst nightmares have come true. I'm flat broke, and my dad is dying.

"I don't know what to do," I wail.

"Chablis, when I was your age, I was workin' in a motel cleanin' up unimaginable filth for pennies. And after my shift, I came home to take care of my two little brothers to the soundtrack of my daddy hitting my mommy. In my free time, I scrubbed the family trailer because I found that, when things are kept clean, people behave more like humans rather than wild animals." She presses her lips together. "Every week, I had two things I looked forward to."

I only know the most basic architecture of my mom's past, so in spite of the bombshells of the last hour, I lean forward. If my mom could bring herself up from a penniless maid to Whip Wainwright's beloved wife, then maybe she could give me some pointers on how to manage my insta-poverty.

"I bought myself a candy bar, and I ate it one teeny, weeny bite at a time, dreamin' of the day when I could buy all the candy bars I wanted." She smiled wryly. "Bless my heart, I didn't realize that, when I could buy all the candy bars in the world, I wouldn't want them anymore."

I picture my mom at my age, wearing an old-fashioned maid's uniform in mint green, nibbling her way through a Mars bar. It's hard to reconcile that image with the well-coiffed woman me who disdains chocolate except for this one variety handmade in a tiny village in the Swiss Alps.

"And after I finished that candy bar, I would take the few coins that people left as tips and put them, one at a time, in a plastic piggy bank my Meemaw gave me when I turned eight. 'Bacon makes dreams come true,' she told me."

"How much money did you deposit every week?"

She shrugs. "Sometimes only a dollar or two, all in nickels and dimes. Other times, it'd be closer to ten dollars." She laughs again, but it's not a happy one. "It sure wasn't because people were generous. They weren't. It was because they were careless. I found the five-dollar bill that fell out of their pants pocket or a handful of quarters they tossed in a drawer and then forgot about. All I did was knock earlier than they expected and stand there with my cart and mop, lookin' official. They'd rush out without lookin' around, and I'd be richer for their haste."

"Did you ever find anything interesting, like a diamond necklace?"

She shakes her head. "It was a motel in coal country. Anyone with a diamond necklace wouldn't have stayed at that podunk place. Mostly it was just used condoms, drug paraphernalia, and tabloids. Lots and lots of tabloids because there's nothin' poor folks like better than readin' about rich folks behavin' badly. I read them myself before I became someone who could be in the tabloids." Her face brightens. "One time, I found twenty dollars. That week, I treated myself to two candy bars, and I chomped them so fast I thought I might get sick."

"How much money did you stash away?"

She preens like a cat. "A thousand dollars. It took me almost three years. I could've done it sooner, but my daddy caught me puttin' in that week's tally—which was all of three dollars. Right in front of me, he picked up the piggy bank, smashed it to smithereens, and then hitched a ride to the ABC to buy himself as many bottles of brown liquor as he could carry."

"That's awful," I say.

"Lucky for me, he found it when I only had seventy dollars in there. Not that I didn't cry for many a day, feelin' that the Lord had wronged me. But like all storm clouds, this one had a silver linin'."

"You learned to hide better."

"That's right. I learned to hide my money and my motivation better." She smiles, but it doesn't reach her eyes. "And boy, did I succeed. When I had my thousand bucks, I walked off my shift and straight to the bus station where I bought a one-way ticket to Las Vegas."

"Why Las Vegas?" Didn't everyone who wanted to get out of their small town go to New York or Los Angeles? Who goes to Sin City unless you want to perform in a kick line while wearing a feathered headdress?

"While I was feedin' my piggy bank, I had lots of time to think.

I'm not talented enough for New York or pretty enough for LA, and Miami, which was my number one choice for a long time, was too dang expensive. Las Vegas had heaps of hotel rooms, and I figured that people indulgin' in cheap booze and high thrills would be careless to leave money around their rooms." Her lips curl upward. "I was right. On my first day, I cleaned twenty-two rooms and scored more than four times that. One room alone yielded me a fancy fifty-dollar bill. It was the first one I'd ever seen up close."

"What were you going to do with the extra money?" I ask. "Now that you'd gotten away from home."

"Do what everyone wants to do. Buy a house on the beach and spend my days drinkin' margaritas while workin' on my tan." Her eyes brighten before the current strain dims them. "But life had other plans."

My stomach twitches with excitement. "You met Daddy!"

She nods. "My roommate, who was all of eighty pounds soakin' wet, had the harebrained idea to enter us into a bikini contest. If either of us won, we'd split the winnings. She had no chance, and I didn't think I had one either, but Whip, who was in town workin' on a deal to get his newspapers into every hotel room in the city, happened to think otherwise."

I squint, trying to see what my dad, then at the peak of his career, had seen in her. She's attractive—people always say we look like sisters except I have my dad's big nose—but she doesn't have drop-dead movie-star looks. She has a nice figure, maintained these days through excessive dieting and intensive exercising—but so do other women. She's smart, but not a scholar; personable, but not charming.

I press my lips together, unsure of why my dad, who could have fallen in love with anyone, chose my mom. She stands to brush the dust off the top of the monitor, and bam—I see it.

She has a spine of steel.

Because she respects herself.

She believed in herself, so much so that she worked herself free from coal country to Las Vegas. She might have only been cleaning hotel rooms, but she knew that if she worked hard that she could lift herself somewhere new. Maybe she couldn't have scaled the stratospheric heights she has without the help of my dad, but I have no doubt that she would have ended up living on a beach, owing nothing to no one.

She is the exact opposite of me.

"So how did a bikini contest lead to you marrying Whip Wainwright?" I ask.

30

"Daddy is a terrible klutz." She stops to smile at me, and for the first time since I got here, it's a real one. "That's where you get it from."

My dad is—I guess *was* would be the better verb since he can't be much of a klutz when he's in a wheelchair—clumsy, but he always made it part of his business acumen. Steak sliding off his fork and onto the table tricked people into thinking he was a no-nothing bumpkin from a North Carolina pig farm rather than a shrewd negotiator. Spilling his glass of water during a board meeting was a way to glance at the notes of others while he pretended to be flustered by the puddles.

"Flaws are assets in waiting," he told me after I'd fallen face-first into my birthday cake at a party for one hundred guests. I'd been thirteen and wearing my first pair of heels, which made my legs wobble like I was a flamingo on ice. I'd run out of the room, crying, my dad hot on my heels.

"You had the entire room's eyes on you," Daddy said. "You could have asked for anything right then and there, and they felt sorry enough for you that you would have gotten it. Instead, you left with nothing but your bruised pride."

I throw my arms around myself at this memory that torches

my heart into an ember of regret. My dad isn't going to be giving me advice any longer.

"Did he bump into you?" I ask. My dad is famous for "bumping" into people he wanted to meet.

She nods. "He was goin' one way, and I was goin' another. I had on an all-white bikini with rhinestone straps." Her eyes go dreamy. "I'd visited all the nice shops to paw through their sales racks until I found the perfect swimsuit. When I put it on, I'd never felt prettier. I saw red when this man, who wasn't payin' a lick of attention, ran right into me. Even worse, he was carryin' a cup of coffee that he dribbled all over my new bikini."

"What happened next?"

I should talk to my mom about the compound, but it's the first time in years we've had a conversation that wasn't about me being a disappointment. So I shelve my thoughts about it. I'll mention it after she's done telling me about how she met my dad.

"I said, 'Do you know how many candy bars I gave up, so I could buy this? And now I don't got a bikini or the candy bars because you're a big old butterfingers."

"And?" I ask in a breathless tone, hanging on my mom's every word. Who knew hearing my parents' origin story would be so exciting?

"He got real quiet for a while before askin' me how many candy bars I'd given up. After I told him how many and how much to the penny, he apologized and sent his assistant to buy me a hundred and two candy bars and a new bikini. I won the competition, and he took me out to celebrate." Her cheeks flush. "It took me a couple of dates before I figured out who he was, but by then, it didn't matter. You were on the way, and we were in love. I would've married him even if it meant livin' in a shack in a swamp."

"You were the first woman to make an honest man out of him."

"Plenty of others tried, but they liked his money more than they liked him. I liked the man because we came from the same upbringin'. We knew what it's like to work hard and value a dollar."

She fixes me with a hard stare. "Chablis, Daddy and I never wanted you to struggle the way we did. We also didn't want you growin' up the way many rich kids do with nannies as parents. That's why we live here, in the middle of Connecticut, where we could be homebodies and enjoy each other. It's why this house has everything we could ever want, so we would leave as little as possible." She sighs. "But I guess too much money is as much a problem as too little. Once you got it in your head that you had a trust fund and could do what you wanted, you stopped carin' about much of anything includin' us. I have shed many a tear about it, but there's nothin' I can do about it these days."

"I'm changing, Mommy. I am."

She crosses her arms. "Chablis, I got a sick husband who can't feed himself and a company on life support I am tryin' to save because, if it's the last thing I do, I'm goin' to make sure Whip lives out the rest of his days in a dignified fashion. It's the least I can do after all the love he showered on me. I don't care—I can't care—if you're changin' or not."

She eyeballs a speck of dirt. "Life sure has a sick sense of humor. When I married Whip, I swore I'd never clean a single thing again." She flicks the dirt away. "Now I'm a maid for the second time in my life." She straightens her spine. "But not for long. And not if I got anything to do with it."

31

M y mom bids me goodnight, and I stumble to my bedroom, the exhaustion sudden and all-consuming. As I push open the door, I smack my forehead.

I forgot to ask my mom about the binder, which is currently sitting under the front seat of the Barbie-mobile. I shrug, remembering the talk with my mom.

It probably doesn't matter. If my dad is an unlikely candidate to fund a compound that trains mass shooters, then my mom is even more so. If a speck of dirt sends her reeling, I can't even imagine what a drop of blood would do to her. Plus, she knows nothing about the media business. To my knowledge, she's never done more than accompany my dad to holiday parties where she made uncomfortable small talk with John's wife, a whisper-thin brunette, who could barely disguise her distaste for my mom's country accent and extreme youth. Running the company for my dad means she's rubber-stamping strategies that have been designed and vetted by John.

I'll tell my mom tomorrow, so she can take care of it or, more likely, tell someone to take care of it for her. Just not John since he's probably the culprit. I exhale. At least that's one less thing for me to worry about.

After flicking on the light, I'm relieved to find that my bedroom looks the same as it has since I was fourteen with its rose-gold walls and framed, signed posters of boy bands. Although it's been a long time since rose gold was my favorite color and my infatuation with shellack-haired boys who sing in counter tenor has faded, the constancy eases my spirit. It reminds me of a time when life was predictable and understandable. I throw myself face first on the comforter and fall asleep with a stuffed rabbit clutched under my arm for comfort.

I wake up hours and hours later in the throes of a nightmare. I'm in a mass shooting, but the person waving a gun is my dad from his wheelchair. I throw my stuffed rabbit at him, but he blows it to pieces. The soft cotton insides swirl around me as I scream at him to stop.

I bolt upright, rubbing the sleep from my eyes and checking the clock beside me. It's early evening. I fall back in bed. Even with the sleep, I'm bone-tired from the drama of the last few days, but my brain, now activated, refuses to let me relax back into slumber.

So I sit up again—reluctantly. I have no idea what to do with myself. Fortunately, my stomach gives me a clue about how to handle the immediate moment. It is grumbling with hunger. Yawning, I walk the quarter-mile it takes to get from my bedroom to the kitchen. It feels like I'm in a haunted house. The rooms are all dark, their furniture covered in white sheets.

Shivering, I throw open the fridge, my stomach twitching in anticipation of the shelves groaning with fresh pasta salads and hunks of cheeses and cut-up fruit just waiting for me to tuck in to.

I blink in shock as I scan the contents. The fridge is empty. Well, not quite empty, but it might as well be. The only thing in it are dozens of meal-replacement shakes.

With that option out, I turn my attention to the cabinets. I paw through them, hoping to find the packages of stone-ground wheat crackers and almond cookies that used to grace their shelves. I swipe my hand over and around, thinking I've missed something, but the only things I find are dust and a few hard brown pellets that make me think of mouse droppings. Feeling desperate, I peer into the recycling bin, hoping it can provide a few clues about what might be available to eat.

My stomach tingles in disbelief. The container is heaped to the brim with empty wine bottles.

I look down my palms as if they might hold the answers to why, all of a sudden, there's a bunch of empty wine bottles. My parents have never been huge drinkers, usually just a glass with dinner, if that. Since recycling comes once a week, this meant someone drank all of these in less than seven days.

Someone must be my mom. I close my eyes. If I'd been around more, she wouldn't have had to shoulder the burden of heading a company and taking care of my sick dad all by herself.

I'll do better in the future, I say to myself. *But first I need food.*

I've got one last place to look. I stand on my tiptoes, so I can peer over the top of the fridge.

"Found you," I say to myself.

My mom has been on a diet for as long as I remember, but she always keeps a box of her favorite chocolates on top of the refrigerator—far enough out of reach that she'll get them only when she's jonesing.

I yank the box down and head to my bedroom. A dozen steps or so later, I stop. Noises are coming from my dad's study. I'm not sure if I'm up for my dad not being my dad anymore, but I creep to the door anyway.

I peek in. My mom is holding one of the meal-replacement shakes to my dad's mouth.

"Please, Whip. Just a sip. For me."

He shoves her off of him. "I don't know who you are, woman."

"I'm your wife." Although I can't see my mom's face, I can hear the tears in voice, the way it quivers as she says wife.

"I don't have a wife."

"Kiss me," she says. "That'll remind you."

My dad haltingly rolls his chair around, so his back is to her. My mom puts her head in her hands, weeping.

"I miss you, Whip. Please come back to me because I need your help. I'm tryin' and tryin' to keep the company alive, but I keep makin' mistake after mistake." Her tears increase. "And to fix those mistakes, I made an even bigger mistake, and I need you to tell me how to make things right because John is of no help. He wants me to fail, so he can swoop in like a buzzard and buy my shares. Tell me, Whip, what should I do?"

"Go away," he growls. "That's what you can do."

Trembling, I run to my bedroom, feeling like I've seen something neither of my parents would have wanted me to see. To push the horrifying scene from my mind, I pop a chocolate in my mouth and then gag. It hasn't quite gone bad, but it's on the way. Shrugging, I chew and swallow. I'm starving, and the only other option is a meal-replacement shake, which means I'd have to go back to the kitchen and I don't want to run the risk of hearing more.

After munching half the box, I succumb to the sugar rush. Which is to say I feel motivated to do something.

I need to get down to the changing-my-life business. But that's going to take some nerves of steel that I can't quite summon right now. Because I'm still a mess. The last week has been more eventful than my twenty-three years combined, but I need to process. I need to forget. I also need to forgive—most of all, myself, for missing what was happening right before my very eyes.

I'm not ready for any of that right now.

I want to have some fun—ASAP. Maybe that'll cleanse my dark thoughts, and I can start fresh tomorrow.

Mind made up, I fire up my ancient desktop. I left my apartment in Austin in such a hurry that I brought nothing with me save the clothes on my back, the binder, and what was in my back pocket: my license, a little cash, and a tube of lipgloss.

As I check my email—nothing more than messages from professors reminding me about final exams and papers—I try to figure out what constitutes fun these days. It's definitely not school work, so I close my email and scroll through a couple of social media feeds.

One post catches my eye. Arthur Schultz-Smith has just checked into a hot Asian fusion restaurant in Tribeca. I pop over to his personal page to see what he's been up. We went to prom together but lost touch the summer after.

Unlike me, Arthur seems to be thriving. He has an MBA from Wharton and is a VP at his family's real estate company. Plus, as I study his profile picture, he's still cute with dark, curly hair and glasses that make him smart rather than nerdy. Best of all, he looks nothing like Colt.

I shoot him a quick message. It takes all of ten seconds before he responds.

I grin. Game on.

Within a handful of minutes, we've arranged to meet at a club I used to love in the Meatpacking district, which leaves me with a small quandary. What do I wear? The clothes I wore home are obviously out of the question because, first, they smell, and second, I couldn't get past the bouncer in them.

I poke through my closet where everything is out of date or too small. I could buy something, but that would involve asking my mom for money and I won't do that.

So I improvise. I wriggle into a pair of black velvet pants, but I can't get them zipped up because puberty happened since I last wore them. So I wiggle out of them and, using a pair of cuticle scissors, I snip through the waistband and put them on again.

I twirl in front of my mirror. Not bad, but I have to cover up the gaping split in the back. I add a blousy minidress that now works as a shirt and, for the finishing touch, scuttle into my mom's closet and grab the first pair of shoes I see. Back in my room, I slip into them and shimmy with delight. They're a pair of strappy designer heels so tall they put my height at close to six feet.

My glee ends when I survey my makeup. All the tubes of lipstick and mascara have expiration dates from five years ago, so I settle for a swipe of lipgloss and call it a day. I scribble a note to my mom and leave it in the kitchen. Just as I'm about to leave, the phone rings shrilly. I grab it fast. I don't want my mom to come in and see I'm wearing her shoes.

"Hello," I say tentatively.

"Libby, could that be you?"

I frown. The voice—soft and manicured like rolling hills at a golf club—sounds familiar, but I can't place it.

"It is."

"John Spencer IV, COO of Whip Media. We've met at various company functions."

The hair on the back of my neck stands up as I remember John and his ice-queen wife, diamonds draped around her neck, glad-handing my dad at a company holiday party. I'd never thought of John as evil, just avaricious, although I'm sure if I pick through my memories, then I'll find what I never thought to look for.

"Yes, John, of course I remember." I go for a frosty, patrician tone as an image of the binder blinks in my mind. The last thing I want to do is talk to him.

"Listen, Libby. I need you to help me. Your father needs you to help me. The company needs you to help it. Something is very wrong with your—"

I cut him off. "Now isn't a good time." Then, I hang up, feeling cold and shaky. I probably should have stayed on the phone with John to see what telling details I could gather on him. Then, when I give the binder to my mom, I can point conclusively to John as the culprit.

But I didn't. Maybe that's okay since I also didn't give any information away. I exhale. For once, by taking the easy way out, I saved myself from a big mess that I'm not prepared to handle at the moment.

With a last look over my shoulder, I leave, my hopes high. Maybe everything that has happened is fate's way of bringing me to the future I'm supposed to be living.

I t takes all of one minute for me to realize that I've made a huge mistake. Actually, huge is an understatement. It is an enormous, incomprehensible mistake.

Because Arthur Schultz-Smith lives up to his initials. He is an A.S.S.

"You're late."

That's his greeting.

"Good evening, and I know." I quickly stuff my parking ticket into the back pocket of my pants. I don't want him to know that I parked in a garage like a regular bridge-and-tunnel person rather than using valet as he did. "Traffic was a nightmare driving from Connecticut."

A.S.S. scowls at me. "I had to wait outside in the elements."

"It's seventy degrees, no humidity, on a clear night. These are the elements that come around three times a year in New York." I laugh, so he knows I'm joking.

"It's not a joke," he says with a pout.

I force myself not to roll my eyes. Up close, A.S.S. is nowhere near as cute as his picture suggested. The curls that looked so fetching before are gnarly with gel, and he has a zit sprouting on his chin. All of that would be fine—for real, I'm the chick wearing pants I had to rip to get on—but his attitude is a big turn off.

But . . . he's also the only option I have right now unless I want to return to Connecticut where my dad is dying and my mom is crying.

So I give it another go.

I throw him a big smile as I step closer. Arthur Schultz-Smith is shorter than I remember, so he's right at the level to appreciate how the minidress-now-shirt clings to my chest.

"I feel like we got off on the wrong foot," I say in my most charming voice. "So why don't we begin again, but this time on the right hand." My play on words is dumb, but I mean the sentiment, so I stick out my hand for him to shake.

He's still frowning like he's put out, but he takes my hand.

"Libby Wainwright," I say as I enthusiastically pump his hand.

He yanks his hand from mine. "You shake hands like a man."

"I'll take that as a compliment."

He snorts. "You're just like your dad."

Hearing him compare me to my dad is like taking a bullet to my already shattered heart, but I would never tell A.S.S. that. Instead, I straighten up and say, "Another compliment. They're like fresh-picked flowers for the soul."

For a moment, he stares at me, his mouth open but with no sound coming out of it. Finally, with nothing to say, he closes his mouth and offers me his arm. We walk into the club. A couple of years ago, this was my favorite place to spend an evening, but I must've changed because it is awful. I recoil from the thumping bass and shriek of fake laughter.

A.S.S. doesn't seem to notice as he maneuvers us to the bar. He tries to ask me what I want to drink, but we're too close to a throbbing speaker for him to understand me. Instead, I gesture for him to order for me.

What he orders is a fishbowl filled with lurid aquamarine liquid. When the bartender pushes it in my direction, I weigh sending it back and ordering myself something of a different hue, like, say, a color found in nature. That, though, would probably result in more "compliments" from A.S.S. so, instead, I sniff it. Expired cough syrup is what comes to mind.

I glance at A.S.S., who is smirking at me. He points at the fishbowl and mimes to drink up. I gingerly take a sip from the skinny straw lolling like a useless buoy in a swamp of toxic waste.

The good news is that it doesn't taste anything like how it looks, which is to say that it tastes exclusively of sugar.

"It's good, right?" A.S.S. screams in my ear. "All the girls love them."

He is drinking a martini with three blue-cheese-stuffed olives on a skewer—a real drink, in other words. With nothing else to do, I suck down half the drink before WHOA. It may taste like a Slurpee, but it hits me like a box of rocks. I start to stagger before I catch myself on the counter.

"Wanna dance," I slur. "I love this song."

I have no idea what song it is I supposedly love since they all sound the same (deafening beats, pitchy vocals). But I need to step away from the fishbowl before I pass out from the dangerous combination of booze and a nearly empty stomach.

A.S.S. follows me onto the dance floor where, together, we attempt some awkward claps, snaps, and step-taps, but we can't get our rhythms to match. After bumping knees a few times, I wedge us into a slow-dance position. It's better, but not by much, as we rock from side to side like we're tweens at our first school dance.

I'm ready to sign off, write the night off as another failed Libby experiment, when something tawny hits my nose.

33

The aroma becomes more potent as I continue to writhe to the heavy beats. My eyes cloud with tears although I keep my smile pasted in place and my hips swinging back and forth.

I don't want to see Colt.

Not now.

Not ever again.

Even though I'm about ten seconds away from bursting into tears, I do the only thing I can think of. I throw myself at A.S.S. I grind up against him as he responds, his excitement poking at my thigh. The D.J. segues into a ballad as A.S.S. tightens his grip on me. I feel absolutely nothing for him beyond vague gratitude for his presence so that Colt didn't find me alone, crying my eyes out for him.

To show Colt that I don't care anymore, I offer my lips to A.S.S. He lifts his head for a kiss, and then everything goes wrong. Our lips connect, but it's my bottom lip to his top because, in my stilt-like heels, I'm taller than him. Quickly, I bend my knees to get our lips to meet correctly, which they do, but the kiss turns from bad to worse. A.S.S. kisses the way he gives "compliments": fast and furious. It feels like my tongue has gotten stuck in the spin cycle of a malfunctioning washing machine.

Normally, I would step away and crack a joke, but since Colt is almost certainly watching, I commit to returning A.S.S.'s tongue scrubbing. Buoyed by my pretend enthusiasm, he doubles down on his efforts, and the amount of saliva he deposits in my mouth increases as a result.

I am kissing A.S.S., I think, thanks to the ridiculous profundity that comes along with too much to drink, so I can make the guy who was an actual ass to me jealous.

I start to laugh, which is a terrible idea because I lose the rhythm of our disaster of a kiss, and A.S.S. chomps down on my tongue. If I had my wits about me, I would have just rolled with it since the nip didn't hurt much. Instead, I flinch, which results in more "compliments" from A.S.S.

"We need to take a step back," A.S.S. says as he moves away from me. "You're moving at a pace that makes me uncomfortable."

A tear spills down my cheek, which he spies.

"I'm just being honest. Radical honesty is the mirror that forces you to confront the ugly truth."

I sigh. "Whatever."

Half-heartedly, I continue to dance, but the space between A.S.S. and me allows another person to slip through. To maintain the travesty that I'm attracted to A.S.S., I rotate myself a quarter turn, which I immediately regret because the tawny aroma becomes unbearable.

Against my will, my eyes find Colt. He's leaning against a column, sipping a beer, not blending in at all in his jeans and boots among the perfumed, label-flaunting clubbers. He, though, doesn't seem to notice or care. His backbone is straight, his expression amused, as everyone around him dances and talks, their desire to be seen and heard dialed up to eleven. When Colt sees me seeing him, he raises his bottle, a small smile playing around his lips.

For one moment, I stare back, hungrily. Then I remember why Colt spent time with me and why he is here tonight—to use me to help himself.

Shoulders slumping, I decide to end this farce of a night. I've changed too much ever to be the person who enjoys clubbing again. I wave at A.S.S., who opens his mouth, but I pretend not to notice. I turn to the exit, which, lucky for me, is in the opposite direction of everyone and everything.

It's time to go back to Connecticut. I'll sleep off this terrible night, and then tomorrow, I'll figure out what's next.

But, of course, life has a sick sense of humor. As I scurry to the exit, tears streaming down my cheeks, I trip over some finance bro, who has his suit-clad legs extended while he yaps on his phone. In my mom's sky-high heels, I waver back and forth, unable to catch my balance thanks to the fishbowl I downed. I fully expect to fall flat on my face, the cherry on this sundae of an awful night, but instead, Colt is there, catching me, his strong, sinewy arms wrapping around me.

"No," I scream although, of course, I mean yes because my heart can't seem to catch up to reality.

"You need better shoes," he whispers in my ear. "But until then, I've got you."

Oh no, you don't, I think.

I push myself up and out of Colt's arms. Standing on my own two feet, I do the only thing that seems sensible. I reach down, yank off one of my shoes, and hurl it at Colt. I'm tipsy, though, plus I'm nothing more than a pulsing, aching nerve, so my aim is terrible.

Colt reaches out and catches the shoe easily. He hands it back to me, but it's too late because I already have the other one in my hand, which I throw at him. This one fares better, landing heel first on his chest. He flinches before grabbing the shoe.

Too late, I realize what a dumb idea that was. Now I'm stuck standing on a floor sticky with what? Spilled drinks? Sweat? I swallow as I acknowledge the other, more likely possibility considering the level of intoxication in the club—vomit.

Rock bottom, I think. That's what this is, standing in the dried, disgusting results of a thousand nights out gone wrong after kissing a guy I don't like and throwing my shoes at the one I do.

Colt extends the ridiculous shoes to me. As I take them, his finger brushes mine, and my heart forgets that this is the guy who used me.

"You need to sober up. Let me buy you a cup of coffee and a slice of pie," he says.

I shake my head. "Not tonight. Not any other night."

His lips turn down at the corners. "We need to talk."

"There's nothing left to be said."

"I can think of something that needs to be done."

I frown. "What's that?"

He doesn't say anything. Instead, he leans down and kisses me. And I can't resist because, when his lips touch mine, I respond. Not as a thinking, rational human, but as a woman who is being kissed by the only man who helped her do more than she'd done before.

I cling to Colt as everything—the noise, the people, the gross floor my feet are stuck to—disappears. What remains is belonging, the idea that, in one person's arms, I can be the happiest I've ever been.

As the kiss deepens, I tell myself this will be it. I will kiss Colt one more time, get him out of my system, and go to Connecticut where I'll put myself together. But that means I have until the kiss ends, so I give myself over to the moment.

And what a moment it is—the two of us bleeding into each together, the soft, silky dance between our tongues.

While I'm still holding my shoes, Colt sweeps me into his arms like I'm a distressed damsel in a Western movie. Dodging all the wannabes, he strides out of the club. Out of the corner of my eye, I see A.S.S., his eyes wide, his jaw dropped, looking like, well, an ass.

See you never, I think as we leave, me swooning in Colt's arms.

34

I take a sip of coffee as the server plunks down slices of key lime pie in front of us. I frown at the fluorescent green wedge, its dollop of whipped cream quivering from the server's manhandling. It looks like someone's idea of key lime pie who's never had real key lime pie, which is supposed to be a mellow yellow hue.

"Pie this color would be a hanging offense in Key West," Colt says as he pokes at the gelatinous mess on his plate.

"Or, at least, being put on permanent litter box duty at the Hemingway house with all those six-toed cats."

Laughing, he clinks his coffee cup against mine. "It's only been a couple of days, but I've missed you, Libby."

"How did you know where I was?"

He winks. "I wouldn't be much of an assassin if I couldn't find you. You never updated your ID to a Texas one, so I already had your parents' address and phone number from booking the plane tickets to Albuquerque. I called and said I was an old friend from Austin. Your mom told me you would be at the club." He half-smiles. "I came even though I hate places like that."

"I used to love them, and now I hate them," I say. "It's like they have to numb people with loud music, dark lighting, and tons of booze for anyone to have fun."

Although he doesn't say anything, the gold in Colt's eyes shines.

Suddenly uncomfortable, I tear my gaze away from him and look around the diner. It appears almost the same as the one in Texas with the jars of ketchup, mustard, salt, and pepper neatly clustered around a napkin dispenser. Motown blasts from the speakers as bright lights bounce off the Formica tables and red leatherette booths. It manages to be both depressing and comforting at the same time.

Colt parks his fork and reaches his hand across the table. He grazes my fingertips with his as I refuse to meet his eyes.

"Why are you here?" I direct the question to the sorry slice of pie in front of me. "I can't imagine it's to talk."

"I came to apologize." His voice lowers. "I also missed you something fierce."

I cross my arms, immediately on high alert. "Nobody flies to New York, so he can apologize to a girl he hung out with for a couple of days." I lean forward. "What do you really want? More money? More information? More access to my dad?"

He jerks a finger at himself. "This guy flies to New York when he knows he's been a jackass." He pauses for a beat to make sure I'm listening. "I'm sorry, Libby. In hindsight, I should have come clean with you in the beginning."

The back of my throat tightens. "You were manipulating me the whole time."

"The truth is more complicated than that. I did suspect someone at Whip Media has been behind the uptick in shootings. Their outlets were always the first to announce them, and they had profiles of the shooters before anyone else. They also used a lot of questionable practices, like focusing on the shooter rather than the victims and their stories." He frowns. "It could be that they had crackerjack reporters and good connections with law enforcement, but the timing was fishy. The pivot came just as the world seemed to be getting more terrible than ever."

"Hasn't the world always been terrible?"

"You would think yes, but the answer is no. Crime has been falling for decades." He laughs without humor. "For a while, I thought I might be made redundant since I went so long between shootings while still getting paid."

He shakes his head. "Then, shootings are everywhere, but why? People might not be intellectually rational, but they're usually emotionally rational. They act out because they're hurting. But there would need to be a lot of hurting to explain why, suddenly, people are shooting up schools, shopping malls, and movie theaters, day after day."

I take a bite of pie and then wish I hadn't. It tastes like sweet glue. Quickly, I swallow it as I process Colt's words.

"What made you think that a media company is behind the increase in shootings, specifically, my family's media company?"

"I followed the money."

My eyebrows raise. "You followed the money?"

"This is America. Profit is motive enough for most things."

"Can you explain?" I hear what Colt is saying, but I don't understand it.

"Someone is benefiting from all those bullets that keep getting shot."

"Gun manufacturers? Firearm advocacy groups?"

He laughs at my suggestions. "They have a clear interest in keeping guns legal, but this type of mass violence could threaten their existence. So no and no."

"But the media benefits?"

"Not all the media. But for someone in the media, yes." He leans forward. "How does your dad make money?"

"Subscriptions, advertisements, selling reader data, sponsored articles . . ." I trail off as it makes sense why a media company, specifically my dad's media company, would fund mass shootings. Particularly since the company was on its way to insolvency, leaving our family broke, which I'll tell Colt about later.

"Whip Media plays both sides," I say. "It always has. My dad said diversity was better for business, that a monolithic viewpoint has no place in a media company. The more divisive an article is, the more eyeballs it gets. All of that adds up to money in the bank."

I look down, getting it. "I see why someone like my dad would benefit from funding . . ." I trail off, not wanting to finish the sentence. "You can't make money if there isn't anything to write about, particularly things that are dramatic and button-pushing. So Whip Media created the content."

Colt nods slowly.

"But it's not my dad," I say quickly, furiously. "I know that for a fact."

His eyebrows shoot up.

I dip my spoon in my coffee and stir as I remember my dad in his wheelchair, how shrunken and old he's become. "He's had a stroke and is suffering from dementia. It's really bad. He doesn't even know who I am anymore." I dab my eyes with a napkin. "I don't think he's here for much longer."

Colt opens his mouth to say something and then closes it. He reaches across the table and takes my hand in his. "There are no good words in a situation like this."

"It's okay," I say over the knob in my throat. "He's lived a good life."

Even to my ears, the words sound fake and forced. Because they are. I said them because those are the words I'm supposed to say, not because it's what I want to say. What I want to say is that my dad is going to die, and all he's ever going to know about me is that I'm a disaster who never got her life together.

For a while, we don't say anything. Colt holds my hand as I stare into my coffee, thinking of everything I would have done differently if I'd known my dad was going to die when I was twenty-three.

Finally, he clears his throat. "In the beginning, I did want to talk to you about Whip Media and see if you knew anything." He holds my gaze. "But then it became about you because I like you more than I've liked anybody. You're special, Libby: lively, funny, game for anything. Good looking, too."

"I paid you," I say. "It was always about the money."

"I know that's what you think, but it wasn't." He reaches into his pocket, retrieves a piece of paper, and pushes it across the table.

I blink as I recognize my handwriting. It's the check I wrote to buy Colt for a week.

"I don't want it," he says. "I want you."

I push it back. "It's for Brian."

"I thank you for that, but no." He grins. "If anything, I should pay you for all the help you gave me. You stopped a potential shooter, sweet-talked him into spilling the beans, and then got us out of danger at the compound with your quick thinking."

Colt takes the check and rips it up. The pieces flutter into a pile in front of us.

"What's next?" I ask.

"I can think of one thing."

My eyes widen. "Which is what?"

"Continue that kiss we had."

I flush, the blood in my veins pumping at double time. I stare at Colt through my eyelashes, remembering the press of his lips against mine, the swirl of his tongue, the heat that built deep inside of me.

He squeezes my hand as my heart pounds.

"But first, I want to earn back your trust."

"Okay," I say, unsurely.

"To do that, I'd like to tell you something I've never told anyone except for the people who lived through it with me."

"Do any of those people know who you are now? What you do now?"

Colt shakes his head. "Outside of the Pact, only you know what I do."

I blink. "Me?"

"It's not something I'm happy about."

E.L. SNOW

I think for a moment, trying to understand. "Because it makes your life small having this job, which has to be completely secret?"

"I don't care about that. I have Brian and my work." He takes his finger and outlines the underside of my chin. "And maybe now, I have you."

"Wha—" I can't think. I most certainly can't speak. All I can do is focus on how the lightest stroke from Colt turns me into an inferno of desire.

He removes his finger and dunks it into his coffee cup before licking it. "Much better now that it tastes like you." He pauses as the air tightens between us. "You're the problem, Libby. Because knowing what I do puts you in danger, and that's the last thing I want. Any time we're apart, that danger ratchets up."

I slump against the hard plastic of the booth. "Oh."

Out of all the men I could have fallen for, why did I have to fall for an assassin? What's wrong with me? It's not the first time I've thought this, considering how I've spent the last several years zooming from disaster to disaster.

Then I look at Colt: the blond hair that swoops low over his forehead, the brownish-gold eyes, and the backbone that is always so straight because he is a man who stands up for what he believes in.

I smile to myself, mentally patting myself on the back. Nothing is wrong with me. He might work on the wrong side of the law, but he is on the right side of morality. With him, I've done more things I'm proud of in a week than I'd done in years.

Colt leans forward, his eyes hard with purpose. "I've thought a lot about whether I should tell you my past or not. It puts you in even more danger. Deadly danger. But I also don't want any more secrets between us."

"I want to know. All of it." And that's the truth, my heart laying it out for me. I want to get closer to, not farther away from, Colt.

He flags the server and points to our cups for a refill. "We're going to need it."

The alcoholic buzz I'd felt in the club has long since faded. I'm wide awake, ready to hear what Colt has to say.

"Are you going to tell me your real name?" I ask.

3 5

"My real name is Christopher Collins although no one calls me that, including my mother, and she's the one who gifted me with the world's most boring name."

"What do people call you?"

He grins. "Chris Cullen."

I laugh. "I like Colt better."

"Me too. That's why I raise no objection to you calling me Colt for as long as you like."

"Why do you have two different last names?"

He half-smiles. "That's part of the story."

"Does me knowing that your real name is Christopher Collins put me in danger?"

"Doubtful."

"Why?"

"It's such a common name that it'd be hard to find the right Christopher Collins. Knowing Christopher Collins' past . . . Now that'll put you in danger."

"Is Cullen Brian's last name too?"

He nods. "We have different fathers. Although, seeing as I never met mine, Brian's dad was the closest thing I had to a father figure.

I went by his last name though it was never made official. Cullen and Collins are close enough that most people didn't notice."

"Why didn't you meet . . ." I trail off. I'm not sure how to phrase my question politely. Fortunately, Colt understands what I didn't ask.

"My mom got knocked up in high school. She graduated one day and had me the next. The guy who did the knocking up left town as soon as she told him, never to be heard from again."

I stroke Colt's hand. "That must have been hard."

"For my mom, yes." He shrugs. "For me, no. It's not like I knew the guy."

"What did your mom do?"

"The same things most young single moms did. She worked two jobs and cobbled together childcare from wherever she could get it, which is to say I was left to my devices in some old lady's house. I would run wild outside while she watched television and poured herself beers after finishing her morning coffee."

"That sounds horrible."

"I don't blame my mom. She couldn't make much more than minimum wage, so childcare had to be cheaper than that for her to have any chance of putting food on the table. If nothing else, I learned to take care of myself from an early age."

I think back to my childcare. My mom was around most of the time, my dad some of the time, and when they weren't available, it was an au pair, who rarely left me alone for more than a minute or two. It's a miracle that I can even tie my shoelaces.

Colt taps the seat next to him. "Mind getting closer?"

I leap up and slide next to him. He tosses his arm over my shoulders and pulls me closer. I feel faint enveloped in his tawny smell. That's the effect Colt has on me.

He buries his face in my hair, and we sit like that for a few minutes, our bodies stuck together, our hearts conversing.

Finally, I pull away, not because I don't like what we're doing—I do, *so* much—but because I want to know Colt's story. I want to understand this man who has, so quickly, become important to me.

"When did your mom meet Brian's dad?" I ask to get the conversation back on track.

Colt peels himself off me although he keeps his arm wrapped around my shoulders. "She was a waitress at a diner not too different from this place." He tips his head to our plates. "But with better pie."

I poke at my slice, the green glowing eerily in the lighting. "That's not a high bar to surpass, no offense to your mom's former place of employment."

Colt grins. "None taken. Anyway, Brian's dad was a regular. He had a dairy farm, and he got tired of talking to cows all day. One thing led to another, and they got married."

"Was that a difficult transition?"

"My mom saw it as an opportunity to right her past. She threw herself into being a wife, cooking, cleaning, and making herself pretty for my stepdad. I felt like the third wheel, which I was." He gazes off into the distance as if he's seeing the past. "I took to spending a lot of time in the barn with the cows. After Brian was born, I took him with me. We'd do chores and play hide and seek. When he got tired, I'd read to him."

"Did they know he had Down Syndrome before he was born?"

Colt shakes his head. "It was a shock, and their marriage was too new to handle the fallout. They constantly argued, which gave them a reason to ignore Brian."

"My parents don't believe in arguing. When they would get upset, which wasn't often, they would stop talking to each other."

He arches an eyebrow. "For how long?"

"Up to a week, but never longer. They're both stubborn, prideful people, and they'd wait it out until they'd forgotten what they were arguing about. But they always made up, and in a way, the argument was worth it because they'd be even more in love after it." I scrunch up my face. "Honestly, it was embarrassing to watch. They'd call each other pet names and snuggle and leave little notes for the other one to find."

"There are worse ways to be in the world than that."

I strive to keep my voice neutral since I'm remembering a family that doesn't exist anymore. "I was lucky, way more than plenty of rich kids. Most of them wouldn't spend enough time around their parents to even know if their mom and dad were arguing." I smile without humor. "I spent so much time with them that I was late to rebelling. But once I discovered it, I took to it like a pro."

"Has it ever occurred to you that maybe you're just as stubborn and prideful as your parents? That may be neither you nor your parents were ready for you to fly the coop? They kept asking you to do things they knew you didn't want to do, and you kept making messes, so they would have to come in and clean them up. All of you were conspiring to keep you as their little girl." He caresses my hair. "Growing up is hard."

My insides are too full to say anything.

"But if last week was any indication, you're not a little girl anymore. You're a woman who can take control of any situation." He wraps a lock of my hair around his finger. "Don't let anyone tell you different. You did amazing things, Libby. I was proud to be your partner."

His words make my backbone unfurl into a straight line. I smile at him before remembering he wants to tell me something serious.

"What's the age difference between you and Brian?"

"Close to four years." His voice lowers. "When Brian was a freshman in high school, I was a senior."

"Where in Texas was your stepdad's farm located?"

"A couple of hours north of Austin. It was a place with a big sky and not much else." He laughs. "Cows aren't the brightest creatures in the animal kingdom, but they're good company. They always remember who you are, and they understand moods."

Colt falls quiet as I snuggle closer. I want him to know that I'm here for him regardless of what he tells me.

"Nothing ever happened in my hometown, and I couldn't wait to get out of there. I was going to take Brian, move to Austin, and get a job. I was so close, only a month left of high school, with a job lined up to work at a dude ranch over the summer so I could get the money for a down payment on an apartment." He frowns. "Fate had other plans."

"What plans?"

"Plans that involved a senior storming the school before third period with an arsenal of guns and a couple of homemade bombs."

I gasp.

"Nobody was prepared. It's not like today where schools have lockdown drills, and security guards are stationed at entrances. It was pandemonium."

I shiver, which causes Colt to rub my arms.

"I know it's in the past," I say through my chattering teeth. "But I can't stop thinking about that night on Sixth Street. I was terrified, but like everyone these days, it happens so frequently that I knew it was something that could happen. You didn't even know it could happen."

"I didn't, although I don't know how I could have made a different decision."

"Decision?" I ask. "What kind of decision does anyone make in that situation? To run or to hide? To play dead or to fight? None of them are good. It feels like the luck of the draw no matter what you do."

Colt's skin pales. "I had to make a decision that had nothing to do with the luck of the draw."

I wedge myself near his heart, which is slamming against his chest.

"I would check on Brian after second period. He had been mainstreamed into an art class, and the kids were cruel. They called him a Mongoloid and stole his colored pencils. It was hard for him to understand why they were laughing at him since he doesn't have a mean bone in his body. So I'd swing by and cheer him up as we walked to his next class."

Colt's voice gets even lower. "That day, my girlfriend walked with us." He gazes at me. "She was a lot like you—pretty, smart, always making people smile. Like you, I couldn't believe she liked me. Like you, she was friends with Brian."

I wiggle, not sure what to make of Colt's revelation. He's talking about her in the past tense, which means . . .

"Where is she now?"

Colt's voice disappears to a whisper that I can barely hear. "We ran into the gunman on our way to Brian's next class. He was panting, red-faced, pretty much a total mess, having just taken out the geometry class. For a minute, we all stood there, looking at each other like we'd wandered into a video game. Even with the black trench coat he was wearing, I knew who he was. He was Travis Campbell, my Chemistry lab partner. He was a bit of a loner, but I didn't mind. I'd invite him to play pickup games of poker I organized with my friends at lunch."

My mouth drops open. Because I know who Colt is and what he's about to tell me.

Colt had been at the Stephen F. Austin High School shooting. It was one of the first of its kind, garnering weeks of intense media coverage: interviews with the survivors, specials devoted to the victims, and op-eds discussing everything from gun control to bullied loners. You couldn't go anywhere or read anything that wasn't about the shooting.

"I remember," I say in a shocked voice.

Internally, I wag a finger at myself. Colt had struck a chord with me since our first meeting. How come I didn't put together who he was, still is? His face had made the front page of the major newspapers, including Whip Media's.

"How come I didn't figure it out?" I direct this question more to myself than Colt. I, who never forgot a face, had forgotten this one.

"A lot of time has passed, and there have been hundreds of mass shootings since the first. Plus, I grew about six inches and added bulk. The last time someone recognized me was seven years ago at a gas station in Waco."

"You were the one who had to . . ." I can't make my lips form the word.

He nods. "Pick. That moment—that decision—changed my life."

"The shooter . . ."

"Pointed his gun at Brian and then my girlfriend. 'Pick,' he screamed. 'You can only save one. Which one will it be, Chris?'"

Colt stops talking. I hug him tight to me. The story of the boy being forced to pick between his disabled brother and his cheerleader girlfriend had gripped the media.

I freeze. The movie that Alexander Benoit had been filming was about the shooting. He'd been cast as Chris Cullen, aka Colt, the man sitting beside me. I'm not sure what to make of that beyond fate feels like a snarled web I can't untangle.

"I would rather he killed me and let them live," he says, his eyes glassy. "If I could go back, that's what I would have said. But at the time, I was working on total instinct. I was so used to protecting Brian that I pulled him close. Before I even realized what I'd done, Travis raised his gun and shot my girlfriend. One bullet and her life was over."

A tear snakes down my cheek. "No one should have to make that choice." My voice is choked with sorrow for Colt, for the situation.

"But, to many people, there was a right choice. I chose to save my brother, who has Down Syndrome and would never be anything more than a stock boy at a grocery store. I let the gunman kill my girlfriend, a straight-A student who was going to be premed at UT."

Colt has grown cold to my touch. Although he's trying to control it, he is quivering. I rub his arms with my hands in brisk, heated strokes.

"I got hate mail and death threats from everyone. Feminists wrote articles claiming that my decision reflected how ingrained the patriarchy is. Right-wing commentators said I'd absorbed the leftist agenda, which elevates the weak in favor of the strong. I don't know who was right then. I don't know who is right now."

His blond hair droops in front of his eyes. Gently, I push it out of his eyes.

"I wasn't thinking about any agenda. I was just a scared kid who did the thing he always did—protect my baby brother. And, in the process, I lost my girlfriend. Her parents wouldn't let me come to her funeral. The best I could do was bring flowers to her grave a few days later."

"Is this why you became an assassin? To make sure no one else has to make the same decision?"

He nods. "One of the ironies of the shootings is that my girlfriend's family sued the district for negligence since it didn't have any protocol for dealing with an active shooter. They won, but with the stipulation that the money be distributed among the victims. Brian and I got enough to leave town and move to Austin. I enrolled him in a school for students with special needs. As for myself," he pauses, "I taught myself how to shoot. Being from Texas, I knew my way around a gun, but my skills were middling. If I ever found myself in a situation like that again, I could stop it before someone else had to face what I had to."

"Before the Billionaires' Pact, did you ever stop a shooting?"

"One time, I stopped a stickup at a convenience store, and another time, I saved a sorority girl from getting raped by a group of drunk frat boys. When the Pact came calling, I was as ready as I could be for a job like this."

"Have you been happy as an assassin?"

"The Pact gave me the resources to stop shootings, and I've done it over and over save the last couple of times. I'll never get a medal for it, but I'm happy that a lot of people are still alive because of me and the Pact."

"What does the world think happened to Chris Cullen? Especially since Alexander Benoit was playing the movie version of you?"

"The world started to care again when the movie was announced, but the Pact put just enough information out there to put off any further inquiries."

"What kind of information?"

"Let's say that they released a picture of me as a dairy farmer in rural Texas. It had been photoshopped to make me look sixty pounds heavier. Plus, they blacked out most of my teeth. I was too much of an eyesore for anyone to come calling. Ugly people don't sell newspapers."

"So you walk through the world invisible these days?"

"Marvin Martins at your service."

Colt locks eyes with me. "So now you know who I am."

And I do know him, these revelations the ones I needed to understand him. I respect him for what he has done and what he will continue to do.

"Thank you for telling me," I say.

"As I said, I don't want there to be any more secrets between us anymore."

"I've got news," I announce.

"What's that?"

"I'm broke. Whip Media is next to bankruptcy, and my trust fund is a joke."

"I know you care about that, but I don't."

"You don't?"

He points at my pie and coffee. "Seems like we do just fine in humble places like this."

As my heart swells, I pull him as close as I can, burying my face in his chest. "What's next?" I say into his collarbone. "Where do we go from here?"

He inches away from my embrace. "I know where I'd like to go from here, but there's unfinished business."

"Unfinished business?" I can't keep the disappointment from

seeping through my voice. I'd been hoping we could head straight to bed for between-the-sheets fun.

"I called in the information about the shooting planned in Tucson at the golf tournament. Do you know what happened?"

I shake my head.

"A whole lot of nothing."

"Didn't the Pact stop it?" Although I've been cooped up in my parents' home, news about mass shootings travels fast, so I would have heard if there'd been one.

"They would have, but there was nothing to stop."

I smack my hand against my head. "The char*mah* must have changed the schedule after he saw us."

Colt nods. "Which makes things worse. Those kids are on a bus with stops planned around the country to kill innocent people, yet we don't know where they're going or who they might kill. You're the only person with the access and knowledge to find out who's behind this, so the Pact can stop them before more lives are lost."

I close my eyes, remembering how close I'd come to losing my life when, what had started as an average day, ended in chaos and bloodshed. I don't want anyone to go through that.

"Do you know how Babe is?" I ask.

"He's well. He gave the Pact all the information he knew, but it ended up being outdated," he says. "Are you sure it's not your dad? He has dementia, and that can lead to a confused sense of reality. He could have arranged it, not understanding what he was doing."

"If you'd seen him the way I did, you'd know he wasn't capable of anything like this."

Although I say the words with confidence, in my head, a small seed of doubt has been planted. Maybe it is my dad, after all, dementia leading him to do things he would never do otherwise.

"That means it's someone else." He pauses to let the words sink in. "Do you want to find out who that is?"

I nod slowly. "I could try. My mom is running the company from home, so I could poke around her office to see if I can find anything." I frown. "I'm not sure what I should look for, though. I already have the signed check that points to my dad."

"Compare signatures on the documents you find," Colt says, his voice low and urgent. "If your dad has been ailing for a while, then his signature will have been in decline as well. Find something he signed a couple of years ago and see how it matches the signature on the check. If and when it doesn't, keep digging. Whoever is behind this must be high up in Whip Media. They're bound to have signed something else." He grins wryly. "Even in the digital age, we still have to put pen to paper to make things legal."

I fidget with my earring. "What if I find something?" For whatever reason, I'm nervous about rooting through my mom's office. It feels like a betrayal of my family. Plus—and even worse—what if it is my dad? I can't turn him in to the police, can I, so he can rot in jail, not knowing who is or where he's at?

I can't. I won't. He's an old man about to die.

"Grab the evidence and run. I'll be waiting for you." Colt glances at me as my eyes tell him all my fears. "If it's your dad, the Pact will figure something out since he's old and sick. They won't turn him over to law enforcement and make him go to jail."

"What would they do?"

"Considering they're all billionaires, I bet they'd stage a takeover of Whip Media and remove him and your mom from the board."

Since I'm already broke, this doesn't sound like a terrible outcome. At least my dad would die with dignity, and my mom could sell everything and start again.

I exhale. "I'll do it."

Under the table, Colt passes me his gun. "Take this."

I eye it suspiciously. "Why would I need a gun? I'm rifling through papers. Even if my mom catches me, I can make up an excuse."

Colt's face goes hard. "I don't think you understand the danger you're in."

"It's my mom," I say. "Not a coldblooded killer."

"Whoever is behind this is savvy. Don't underestimate them or the situation. Just because it's not your dad doesn't mean it isn't someone your dad trusts and cares about." His tone is urgent. "Keep it on you at all times."

Sighing, I reach for the gun and tuck it into the waistband of my pants. It slips neatly into the rip in my pants.

Colt shrugs out of his jean jacket. "Take this too."

"Why?"

He points at the lump of the gun through my top. "So you can keep that hidden."

For a moment, I forget everything as I push my arms through the sleeves of the jacket. It's warm and smells like Colt. I luxuriate in it, feeling like even the most expensive fur wouldn't feel as wonderful as wearing his jacket.

"Do you need anything else?" he asks.

Shaking my head, I take the last swig of my coffee. It's go time.

Colt grabs me and draws me close. He kisses me hard and fast before pulling away. "Be careful."

On the way back to Connecticut, I imagine what would happen if it were my dad, his dementia leading him astray from his strong moral code. Obviously, I would have to do the most heartbreaking thing a daughter could do to him—divest him of the company he built from a one-newspaper operation into a media empire.

But I can't let innocent people die no matter how much I love my dad.

I cross my fingers that it's somebody other than my dad. I haven't been to a company holiday party in years, so I have no idea who the current top brass is beyond John. In the past, all the high ranking players had been similar to John, wearing big grins with sharp teeth.

If it's not John, then it's one of those sharks. It's just a matter of a little detective work to identify which one.

But I'll find you, I say to myself as I pull in to the driveway. After grabbing the binder, I stop and gaze at the home that held so many happy memories. Now, though, it seems like a haunted house with all the lights out. Not even the lanterns by the front door are on.

Once inside, I kick off the ridiculous heels and pad to my

mom's area in my bare feet. Colt is right. I do need better shoes, ones that allow me to move without peril.

As I pad down the dark hall in bare feet, my confidence slips as I pass by my dad's study. I peek in, then wish I hadn't. He's asleep on the cot, a blanket pulled up to his chin, his wheelchair parked beside him. In slumber, he looks as small and helpless as a baby.

My mom has wedged herself between the cot and the wheelchair. She lies over the edge of the cot, her long blonde hair coiling over my dad's legs. The moonlight streams through the window, making the huge diamond on her ring finger glint menacingly and the crumpled tissues strewn around her glow eerily. An empty wine bottle rests next to her, and the blonde-ringleted doll from earlier is in her lap. That's weird, but it's a weird time and I don't want to judge whatever brings her comfort although her drinking is worrisome.

For a moment, I stare at them, tears pushing at my eyes. Lots of people have claimed that my mom was a gold digger, marrying Whip Wainwright for his money, but they were wrong. She loved him then, and she loves him now, even though he doesn't know who she is.

I close my eyes. I truly hope my dad isn't behind this. It would devastate my mom and me.

I give them a last look, imprinting what true love looks like on my heart, before wrapping Colt's jacket around me. Although it's warm outside, it's cold inside, the dark, empty hall unheated by bodies or conversation.

I hurry to my mom's study. Once there, I push open the door with misgivings, half expecting to see whoever's behind this sitting at my mom's desk.

Instead, no one and nothing is there, save the strong lemon scent of furniture polish. I look around, unsure of where to start my hunt. Shrugging, I grab the nearest stack of papers and start going through them.

After a few, my eyes glaze over. They contain nothing exciting, just oodles of contracts and memos. The ones that require a signature have my mom's, her letters loopy, all the W's flourished with a curlicue. I go through another a different stack and then another, but I can't find anything with a signature other than my mom's. From the dates, it appears my mom has been standing in for my dad for a while now. After thumbing through the stacks twice, I concede defeat.

I tap my foot. Should I give up and tell Colt I can't find anything?

I like this idea more than I should. I turn to leave, my body wilting with relief.

Then I remember the thump of dead bodies, the shrieks of terror, looking into the man named Greg's lifeless eyes as his wife sobbed over him.

I can't quit.

Plus, there's another place I can look—my dad's study. Although he hasn't been running the company for a while, I'd bet his file cabinets contain plenty of old documents. I'll have to be super quiet since my parents are asleep in there. If I don't find anything, then I can quit with the confidence that I did try everything.

Once in the study, I risk bringing up the lights just enough so that I can see the words. My parents are still arranged in their tableaux of marriage vows made real: for richer, for poorer, in sickness, and in health.

A whirring sound makes me jump. Making my face blank, I turn to face the noise before laughing to myself. It's a small space heater that's angled at my dad.

Feeling safe, I pull open the first file cabinet, going as slow as I can. Even still, it creaks. I wince and glance at my parents. They're still asleep, thank goodness.

I exhale as I comb through the documents. Most of them are dated ten years earlier, my dad's signature strong and firm. Unlike my mom's Ws with their loops, the W in his Whip and Wainwright trails straight and high.

I grab a contract to compare to the one in the binder as sweat beads on my temples. The space heater is giving off more warmth than its small size suggests. I take off Colt's jacket to cool myself.

I kneel to open the next file cabinet, which lays under the first. The gun, though, pokes me in the leg. Sighing, I stand and place it on top of the jacket. Colt's warning pings in my head—keep it on you at all times—but this situation doesn't count, does it? I'm the presence of my sleeping parents. I'm as safe as I can be. Plus, wouldn't it be worse if, while I'm kneeling, the gun falls out of my jury-rigged pants and wakes everyone up.

I kneel again and start going through the paperwork. As I rummage through the files, my chest aches. My dad's signature tells the story of his decline. Each year, it gets shakier and harder to read. Sometimes, it isn't even on the line or it has a strange start, the letter looking nothing like a W. The documents from a couple of years ago are the worst, scribbles that cover the page and don't resemble letters.

Although this tells me everything I know—my dad is not the person who funded a compound of killers —I do my due diligence. I compare several of the contracts to the check in the binder.

The check's signature matches the contract from ten years earlier, but it doesn't look anything like the toddler scrawls of the latest signatures. I move my eyes back and forth between the contract and the check. Someone signed it for my dad, and they did a pretty good job.

With my index finger, I trace the letters on the contract and then the check. It takes me twice before I gasp out loud. It's so small that I wouldn't have noticed it if I hadn't studied hundreds of documents with this handwriting quirk. The W of Wainwright has a curlicue before the pen skips to the strong, bold strokes of my dad's signature. The writer defaulted to her normal habits before remembering who she was supposed to be impersonating.

To be sure I'm not seeing things, I line up a contract my mom signed next to the check. I sketch the curlicue of the W as I hope, hope, hope I'm wrong.

I'm not.

The curlicues match.

I check again and again, but the result never changes.

Mechanically, I shove the contract into the binder and stand up, my heart feeling like it's about to pop out of my chest. I press the binder against my ribs as I try to figure out what I'm going to tell Colt.

"Chablis."

I turn around, a thousand excuses ready to tumble out of my mouth.

But I can't think of a single one when I see my mom. She has Colt's gun pointed at me.

39

"You're pointing a gun at me," I croak, stating the obvious because I don't know what else to say.

In all my wildest ideas about who would be behind the compound, not one featured my mom. Not one involved her aiming a gun at me.

Yet here we are. I tighten my grip on the binder.

My mom waves the gun. "Give it to me. Now."

I shake my head. I have no idea how I'm going to extricate myself from this situation, but I can't leave without the binder. If I do, then I'll have lost the proof that exonerates my dad and . . . implicates my mom.

"Why?" I ask. In that one word, I phrase all of my questions.

"Why what?"

"I know, Mommy."

"Know what?"

"That you funded a compound to train mass shooters."

Although my mom doesn't budge, she pales.

"You have lost your mind," she says.

"If I've lost my mind, then why would you care if I have this binder?"

"I can't let you take company documents out of this house." My mom goes for bravado, but she knows and I know that the effort is wasted.

"You made a mistake with the signature on the check to the compound," I say.

She presses her lips together. "That's not exactly goin' to incriminate me. After all, it's Daddy's signature on the check."

I gesture to the file cabinets behind me. "Daddy's signature has been declining for years. No one will believe he signed this." I hesitate. "Plus, I know he would never do anything like this, even in his current state. Why, Mommy? Why did you do this?"

"Because nothin' else was workin', and I was gettin' desperate."

"But funding a compound to train mass shooters? That's not desperation. That's insanity."

"When I took over for Daddy, I thought I was the perfect gal for the job. I'd spent years reading tabloids and trashy magazines, and I knew what people want—pulp. But there's not enough pulp to go around, and on the occasion when there is, the cycle is short because so many media outlets are desperate for news these days. I tried making up news for a while, but people cottoned on too quickly. Once you're known as a liar in the business, the only people who will come around are cranks, and advertisers hate them. So, I figured if I made the news from scratch, then Whip Media could be the first to report it. Mass shootings will always be the biggest news there is, and there are so many angles that one can be made into a week or so's worth of news."

She smiles although it doesn't reach her eyes. "Folks love the personal angle, particularly stories about the shooter. They get more traffic than profiles of movie stars."

"But you're killing innocent people."

I can't wrap my head around it. My mom—the woman whose biggest decision for years was what color to paint her toenails—thought that killing innocent people was a good business decision.

"Chablis, do you know what kind of dire straits we're in right now?"

"I know we're broke."

"Broke means you don't got money. We don't got money, and we owe a whole mess of it. If I don't turn the company around, I'm goin' to lose the shirt on my back and go back to being a maid in coal country." She waves a hand around the room. "Poof. All of this gone like it never happened."

"When did it get so bad?"

"It was already startin' to get bad when I married Daddy." She laughs without humor. "Isn't that a hoot? Everyone called me a gold digger, but most of the gold was gone at that point because Whip wasn't made for business in the 21st century. He didn't tell me for the longest time, letting me run up huge credit card bills while I was spoilin' you rotten. But there was always money to borrow, and as long as Daddy had his senses, he could rob Peter to pay Paul and then rob Paul to pay Peter. Once he started to lose his memory, though, that's when we started bleedin' red all the time."

"Can't you sell some of your jewelry or something? Why would you pay people to kill other people?"

My mom laughs and laughs. "Sell my jewelry? You don't think I've done that and a whole lot more?" She points at her ring. "This is all I got left. I'd sell it too, but every once in a while, Daddy comes back, and it gives him comfort to think nothin's changed." She waves a hand around the room, pointing at the custom-made drapes in thick maroon velvet and heavy furniture adorned with lion heads. "Nothin' is worth anythin'. That's the problem with trying to sell all this expensive junk. Everything is one-of-a-kind, and that means no one wants it because it's my taste, not theirs." She glares at me. "I even sold shares of the company to John, which would break Daddy's heart. I hemmed and hawed over that decision for almost a year before biting the bullet. Of course, they weren't worth much, so all that grief for a few piddly dollars."

"Why not declare bankruptcy?"

"Because I came into this world with a pine drawer for a cradle, and I don't plan to go out with a pine box as my casket. I'm smart enough to do it. I just need time and a little luck because I know this world."

"What world is that?"

"We live in angry times. Folks like name callin' and yellin' at each another. It makes them feel good about themselves and distracts them from their troubles. I know this because I grew up poor, and plenty of poor folks—and not-so-poor folks, too—like being angry. It gets them going, which gets them through their day."

"And mass shootings make people angry?"

She shakes her head. "Arguing about how to stop mass shootings makes people angry, and angry people are good for business because they keep reading and responding. Advertisers love them because they're easy to target. And I love advertisers."

My mom re-aims the gun at me. "Now give me that binder."

40

I press the binder flat against my chest. It won't stop a bullet, but it might slow it down a little.

"You're not going to shoot me, are you?" I ask through my chattering teeth.

"I will point this gun at you until you give me that binder." She sighs. "You could have been a good girl, Chablis. Gone to college, gotten a job, married someone nice. But you wouldn't go to class, so we're here."

"I didn't plan on walking into a mass shooting." Then, a thought so horrible I barely entertain it pops into my head. "Did you know that I was going to be there?"

"You're my only child. Of course, I had no idea."

"Was Sixth Street one of yours?"

She shakes her head. "That was by a deranged guy whose girlfriend was the president of Alexander's fan club. He thought she spent too much time moonin' over Alexander."

I exhale. At least this is something, which isn't much of anything, considering the extent of my mom's crimes.

"Once you told me you'd been there, I got Ximena and Orpita to scamper on over. That's when I knew there was goin' to be trouble sooner or later."

"How?"

"I had them take a picture of the gentleman who saved you, so I could check him out. It took one look for me to figure out who he was—Chris Cullen, that boy who chose to save his brother with Down Syndrome over his pretty, smart girlfriend. Who could forget that story?"

"You've got a good memory," I say.

"I never forget a face. Daddy used to say I should have gone into politics."

"Why did it matter if it was Chris Cullen?"

"I didn't need to know why it mattered. I just knew it did. I had Ximena and Orpita follow you the next day."

So I had seen them when Colt was driving us to visit Brian.

"While they did that, I did some research on this Chris Cullen, who you seemed so smitten by."

"What did you find?" I cross my fingers that she didn't find more than the picture the Pact released of him.

"Being the head of a media empire, even if it's crumblin' into dust around me, does have its perks. I used facial recognition software to go through all the photographs Whip Media has." She smiles although it doesn't reach her eyes. "Technology is amazin'. It only took a couple of minutes before I realized Chris Cullen had a flair for showin' up at mass shootin' after mass shootin'. I'd say that's pretty bad luck unless he had another reason for bein' there. So I tested that idea out with a pretend shootin' at UT."

"You were behind the kid?"

She nods.

"I was there, Mommy."

"I had a feelin' you might be. His guns had been jury-rigged to jam, so no one would get hurt."

"Then what was he supposed to do with that gigantic arsenal?"

"Lure Chris Cullen to the campus." My mom sighs. "Which he did although nothin' else went to plan."

"What do you mean?"

"I mean that he was supposed to lure Chris Cullen to campus

where one of my people would be on-site to question him. Instead, that boy vanished into thin air. But it didn't matter much because I'd already guessed why Chris Cullen was showin' up at mass shootings so regularly. He was tryin' to stop them."

I freeze. Does my mom know about the Pact?

"Do you think he's working for someone?" I try to keep my tone as casual as possible.

"I doubt it. But he's a young man on a mission that is directly opposed to mine." She narrows her eyes at me. "I'd bet there's a reason why he's suddenly so interested in the daughter of Whip Wainwright."

For the first time since I turned around to find my mom pointing a gun at me, I feel like I'm on firm ground. I already know this.

I sniff and pretend to blink back tears. "You think he was using me?"

"I'd bet he was usin' you to find out more about us."

"But he said he likes me."

She rolls her eyes at me. "You sure are gullible."

"He followed me here after we had a fight."

My mom cocks her ear to me. "A fight about what?"

Thinking fast, I blurt, "My money. I thought that's why he liked me."

"Well, he wouldn't be the first."

"But then I told him that we're broke, and he said he didn't care."

"Does he know about your trust fund?"

I nod slowly.

She laughs meanly. "He cares. It might not be much to you or me, but it's got to be a lot to a guy who grew up on a dairy farm."

And just like that, my mom has sent me spiraling into my insecurities.

"Did you know it was Col—Chris, I mean—who called for me?"

"Of course. And I sent him to you."

"Why?"

"Because I needed to get a plan in place, seeing as I had a busload of shooters and nowhere to send them after your escapades at the compound."

"A plan in place?" I echo.

She jiggles the gun to a remote control on the desk. "Flip on the TV. Any old channel should do the trick."

Although it's warm in the bedroom, I shiver as I reach for the remote to turn the television on. The screen flares to life, showing a boring, beige apartment complex in Round Rock, Texas. I don't need to read the bottom of the screen or to listen to the announcer tell me what's going in because I know who's in danger.

"Brian!" I scream. "How could you?"

"You see, Chablis, I had a feelin' Chris Cullen would sweet talk you into doing his dirty work. He's nice-lookin', and Ximena and Orpita told me it'd been a good long time since you've had a man in your life."

"He didn't sweet talk me into anything. I wanted to find out who was funding the compound."

"You keep tellin' yourself that." She points the gun to the television where the news announcer is talking about how a gunman is loose in an independent living facility for special needs adults. "But when things go from bad to worse in there, you think long and hard about who you want to blame."

"What do you want?"

"For starters, I want you to give me that binder. Then, you walk out of here and don't look back. Once you've done that, I'll call it off."

"How are you going to stop me from going to the police and telling them what you know?"

She raises her eyes heavenward. "You think they're goin' to believe you? You got no proof."

"I know where the compound is."

"No, you don't," my mom says. "After I heard about your little visit, I paid a pretty penny to have it burned to the ground."

With the binder still to my chest, I clasp my hands in a pleading gesture. "Don't do this, Mommy. Please."

"The way I see it, you're the one who's got to pick. Do you want Chris Cullen's little brother to live or to die?"

I don't say anything, just beg her with my eyes. I have no idea what to do. Should I let a gunman kill Colt's brother or let my mother have the binder, which is the only proof of who's behind the mass shootings?

"The longer you hold on to that binder, the more likely real harm is goin' to come to those folks. The gunman is a kid, after all. How long do you think he's goin' to hold them hostage before he gets tired and lets loose?"

"Chablis," a warm, resonant voice says. It's one I thought I'd never hear again.

41

My jaw drops as my dad pulls himself to sitting on the cot. His eyes look bright, his expression lucid. His mind must have cleared. For at least a minute. Hopefully more.

Poor Daddy. I can't even imagine what this scene looks like to him. My mom is pointing a gun at me as a potential mass shooting unfolds on the television screen.

He runs a hand through his white hair. "What on earth is going on?" My heart clenches at the familiar gesture. I remember it from my youth, something he did a thousand times when he was confused.

"Whip," my mom exclaims.

She rushes to my dad, lowering the gun as she does.

Time screeches to a halt. I have two options. I can take the gun from my mother, or I can hug my dad, this probably being my only chance to tell him how much I love him while he's in possession of his faculties.

My mom flings the arm that's not holding the gun around him and buries her face into his chest. My dad rains kisses on the top of her head. They look like a couple who has been reunited after a long absence.

I shift my eyes to the gun, which is loosely grasped between her fingers, her arm hanging by her side.

It is now or never.

I dash over and yank the gun from her hand.

She and my dad look up, startled, to find me pointing the gun at them.

"Hi, Daddy," I whisper. "I've missed you so much."

"Where did you get an original Colt SAA Peacemaker from?" he asks. "And, for heaven's sake, why are pointing it at us?"

"It's a long story." I tighten my grip on the gun before moving it until it's aimed at my mom. "Why don't you have her tell it?"

She pales. "Chablis and I had a little misunderstanding, that's all."

I laugh incredulously. "A little misunderstanding? That's what you're calling it?" I jerk the gun to the television. "You ordered a gunman into a facility where special needs adults live. You trained that gunman at a special compound funded by Whip Media. This isn't even the first time you've arranged a mass shooting. You've been ordering them to create content to appease advertisers."

My dad's mouth flops open as his eyes widen. I immediately regret my decision to drag him into this since this is the first lucid moment in a long time. But what else am I supposed to do? Sweet, innocent Brian is being held hostage along with a bunch of others who've never hurt a fly in their lives.

My dad directs his gaze to my mom. "Tell me, honey," he says. "Everything."

"Oh, Whip. You left me in charge of a company that was already dead." She dabs at her eyes as he pulls her closer. "The only way to bring it back to life was to do something real extreme."

And then the whole story comes tumbling out. We had debts up to our eyeballs, a board that wanted to declare my dad incompetent, the loss of my dad as her one and only friend, a daughter who never called or visited, a lot of drinking to ease the pain of losing everything she loved. One night when everything felt so dark and hopeless that she was contemplating ending her life when her email pinged. The sender was anonymous, but my mom now suspects it was John Spencer IV. She opened the email, and a conversation developed between her and someone who called themselves Becky. Becky claimed to be an administrative assistant at Whip Media, who had met my mom a couple of times and thought she was nice. She reached out because she thought my mom might need a friend. Night after night, my mom spilled her feelings, confessing about the extent of my dad's illness and the precariousness of the company. Becky introduced her to a few business associates on the deep web who might be able to help her if she didn't mind an unorthodox business venture. Once there, a plan was laid out for lifting the company's sagging revenues, which, after they turned around, the Becky said John would buy a few of my family's shares at top-dollar to help us get liquid again. The company, though, would still belong to the Wainwright family. All my mom had to do was follow the instructions before cashing out at the very end. Drunk and desperate, she agreed. The plan worked, and as for all the times her conscience bothered her, well, she'd have another glass of wine to shut it up.

My dad doesn't say anything as my mom is talking. This is another one of his business strategies. If you let someone talk long enough, you'll gather enough to one-up them.

"Do you have any proof of these conversations? A printout of the emails? Maybe saved to a folder on the computer? Anything that would point to John or someone else at the company?"

She shakes her head. "I didn't think about doin' that for the longest time, and when I did, all the emails were gone. It was like I'd made it all up although I know I didn't. It happened. I know it did."

My dad sweeps his eyes to the doppelganger doll by his cot and then meets my eyes. He says nothing as do I, but our thoughts are the same. My mom has become unhinged due to the stress.

She collapses beside my dad, tears streaming down her cheeks. "I didn't want to do it, Whip, I swear, but I didn't know what else to do. I thought if I could save the company, then I'd have the money to get our life back on track. I could take you to specialists to get you the help you need. Chablis would graduate college. We would be a family again, and you'd be proud of me for turning things around."

My dad stares deep into her eyes as I tap my foot, my worry increasing by the minute. The longer it takes, the more likely it is that the gunman is going to start shooting.

"Daddy, there's a hostage situation going on right now," I plead. "Do something."

He says to my mom, "End the hostage situation. Then, I'll tell you what we're going to do."

She punches some numbers into her phone. "Done." Her voice has the parched sound of someone who is all cried out.

For several tense minutes, we wait, gazing at the television. Then, the screen fills with the jubilant face of an anchor.

"I've just received word that the situation has been defused by a heroic individual who talked the gunman down."

Out of the boring, beige apartment complex, the residents file out. I whoop when I see Brian, who looks dazed but, otherwise, no worse for the wear. The camera cuts to an image of—

Oh, no. That can't be who saved the day via my mom's command. On-screen, the charm*ah* is grinning evilly. My stomach sours. He's even grosser up close and on television, his eyes like two tiny black holes in a wrinkly bag of a face.

"It was the only out I had," my mom says tiredly as she sees my horrified face. "He's god awful, and he'll see another day of bein' god awful, but at least everyone is alive."

You're god awful.

It seems impossible that my feelings could flip so quickly from love to hate, but the magnitude of my mom's actions leaves no room for any other reaction.

I place the gun on the seat of my dad's wheelchair. At this point, everything is in the open and Brian is safe. Although I miss the control and power its heft provided me, I want my dad to stay coherent, and I don't think waving a gun around will do that.

My dad points to the place beside him on the sofa. I plop down as he wraps his arm around me. He gazes first at my mom and then me, his eyes so sad.

"I'm sorry," he says. "The problems may not end with me, but they certainly start with me. I was old and pigheaded, and I should have sold the company years ago to John. He was the whippersnapper with all the ideas. Instead, I held on to it, and then I asked you to hold on to it when it wasn't worth holding on to."

He drops a gentle kiss on my mom's forehead. "I remember how I said many times, 'I may die, but my company will live forever.' And I told you, 'Do anything and everything to keep the company in our family.'" He shakes his head ruefully. "And now we're in a horrible mess."

I keep my mouth shut, but I'm not sure my dad understands precisely the magnitude of my mom's crimes. She should go to jail, for a long, long time.

"Chablis."

I startle.

"Hand me the phone."

I pass it to him, my hands shaking. I have no idea what he's about to do.

With sure, steady strokes, he punches three digits into the phone: nine, one, one.

"Hello," he says, his voice as calm as an ocean after a storm. "My name is Whip Wainwright, and you need to send someone to arrest me. I've committed a terrible crime."

42

The three of us sit huddled together as we wait for the police to arrive. With his arms around my mom and me, my dad talks in a low, soothing voice about happier times.

"Do you remember Chablis' eighth birthday when we went to Disney World? We ate ice cream for breakfast, cake for lunch, and cookies for dinner."

Neither my mom nor I say anything even though there is so much I want to say. My mom holds the doll in her lap and lays her head on my dad's chest. I burrow into his side as my heart grapples with the truth. My dad is going to sacrifice himself for my mom. Although it is romantic, it certainly isn't right.

Sooner rather than later, sirens peal up the driveway. My dad stops his monologue as my mom starts crying.

"Chablis," he whispers in my ear. "Your mother has lost her mind. Call the lawyer and have her committed to a mental hospital. Make it as cushy as you can, so she'll stay. Sell everything, including the company, to make it happen." He gives me a searching look, his bushy white eyebrows pushed together. "Are you going to be okay by yourself?"

I push back the tears beating at my eyes. "I'm going to be just fine, Daddy. I've stopped respecting my circumstances and started respecting myself."

He squeezes me before turning to my mom. "You need rest, honey. Chablis is going to arrange that for you. Promise me you'll do what she says."

My mom nods robotically as the police bang on the door.

What happens next is a blur. My dad confesses to a crime he didn't commit as my mom and I look on. The police, three men and one woman who has more muscles than her other colleagues combined, listen before reading him his rights. They settle him in his wheelchair, and my dad, his face tight and grim, holds out his arms for handcuffs.

It's ridiculous, really. My dad can't walk anymore, so I'm not sure what the handcuffs are for, but I keep my mouth shut. Something tells me that's the best thing I can do. The sight is almost unbearable. My dad—so thin, so old, so broken—is going to spend his last moments on earth in a jail cell.

I berate myself, playing the scene between my mom and me over and over. If only I'd found a way to disarm her or maybe made a run for it or had just kept the gun on myself, then I could have told Colt. The Pact would have saved my dad from this terrible end to a wonderful life.

My mom's words start running on repeat in my head because I know she's right. If I'd done what I was supposed to do—go to class on my birthday—then none of this would have happened. I would have remained blissfully ignorant of my mom's horrible choices, and my dad would have died in peace. Instead, I had to go chasing after a guy, and now I'm here, watching my dad getting arrested for a crime he didn't commit.

Just as they're about to wheel him out of the room, my dad straightens up.

"I love you both," he says and then collapses.

"Whip!" my mom yells as she runs to him.

The female police officer steps in front of her, but my mom

pushes her away with superhuman strength. She throws herself at my dad, wailing.

"Come back, Whip, come back."

"Ma'am," the female police officer says. "You need to move out of the way."

My mom wraps her arms around my dad. "You'll have to kill me first."

A cursory glance around the room shows that no one is paying any attention to me. Like a zombie, I walk out wordlessly, refusing to look behind me.

I step out of the front door. Picking up my pace, I run past the Barbie-mobile and down the mile-long driveway. Faster and faster, I go, not caring about the pokes of rocks on my bare feet or the dirt that's burying itself under my toenails. To someone else, they might think I'm running from what's happening inside.

But I'm not, I'm not, I'm not. I'm running to my future where I won't be a poor little rich girl any longer. I'll still be rich, though, but in myself. As for my bank account, I don't care anymore and I never should have in the first place, happiness being unrelated to its number.

The Sixth Street shooting showed me a new way forward. Before it, I'd been alive but dead in so many ways. Now, I've woken up to the possibilities of life.

I exit the gate, and there he is, just like I knew he'd be.

Colt flings his arms open, and I run into them.

"I've been following the news," he says. "Then I saw the cops go in, and I thought you were injured or . . ." His voice hitches. "Dead."

"Did you think you could get rid of me that easily? Brian still hasn't taught me how to make hospital corners."

Although my voice wobbles, the joke feels good. It reminds me that, even with the horrible revelations of the last few hours, life will move forward. As will I.

He laughs before his expression flattens into a serious one. "I would have been devastated."

I brush a kiss against his lips, which he returns—passionately.

When we come up for air, he traces the underside of my chin with his index finger.

"The road before you is wide open, but let me make my case for one route. Go with me to Texas, so I can buy you short rib tacos. Go with me, so I can make love to you on a proper bed. Go with me, so I can tell you every day how much I love you. Go with me, so we can build a future together."

"I'll drive," I say.

THE END

END NOTES

- Truth, as they say, is stranger than fiction. The impetus for *C is for Colt* came from a New York Post article I stumbled upon about a compound in New Mexico that was training kids to be school shooters.
- The idea that a media organization would fund mass shooters stems solely from my imagination; however, certain media practices such as focusing attention on the shooter rather than the victims do increase contagion. More information can be found here (https://health.usnews.com/wellness/health-buzz/articles/2017-02-07/best-practices-offered-for-media-coverage-of-mass-shootings). You can also visit the epigraph page where I list several headlines from different outlets about the compound. Although they convey roughly the same information, you can decide for yourself if the slight changes would encourage you to click on one rather than another or influence your opinion about the content.
- I hemmed and hawed for weeks about Libby's riches-to-rags arc since, in romance, a rising fortune often accompanies love. Yet, as the Beatles sang in their

inimitable song, money can't buy you love. I thought it would be interesting to have a protagonist who loses her fortune yet gains love and self-respect at the end—two things I'd argue are much more important than a hefty bank account.

- In regards to that riches-to-rags arc, it was fun to weave the shoe motif throughout. Libby begins in a pair of fancy gold heels and ends in bare feet—a Cinderella in counterpoint.
- The trolley problem that Colt and Libby discuss is a famous thought experiment. Learn more here: https://en.wikipedia.org/wiki/Trolley_problem.

Thank you for reading *C is for Colt*. **If you have any kind words about your reading experience, then I would be deeply indebted if you could share them on the site at which you purchased the book.** Keep your eyes peeled for *D is for dB*, coming soon. The lowercase d is intentional; can you guess what his weapon is?

If you didn't enjoy *C is for Colt*, I appreciate you taking a chance on an unknown writer. Your time and money are important. May your next reading experience be better.

ABOUT THE AUTHOR

E.L. Snow is a Southerner living in the Northeast, who loves reading, reality television, and rosé wine. Feel free to contact her at ellysnowauthor@gmail.com if you have feedback or suggestions for future installments of ASSASSINZ.

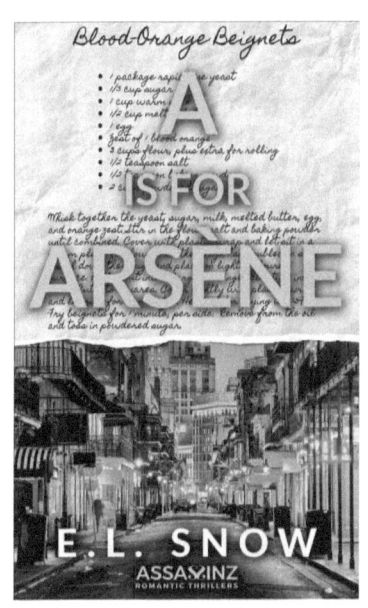

Coming soon

D is for dB